Misfortune and Mystery

In

Mistletoe

Mistletoe Treasures Book 3

By

Ronna M. Bacon

Joshua 1:9

Have I not commanded you? Be strong and of good courage; do not be afraid, nor be dismayed, for the Lord your God *is* with you wherever you go. (NKJV)

Table of Contents

Prologue
Chapter 1
Chapter 2
Chapter 3
Chapter 4
Chapter 5
Chapter 6
Chapter 7
Chapter 8
Chapter 9
Chapter 10
Chapter 11
Chapter 12
Chapter 13
Chapter 14
Chapter 15
Chapter 16
Chapter 17
Chapter 18
Chapter 19
Chapter 20
Chapter 21
Chapter 22
Epilogue

The little girl's cries split through the night as she wept for her parents, for her own bed, for her stuffed dog. The woman in the front seat stared at her dispassionately before she turned around once more, her conversation with the male driver uninterrupted.

The little girl finally slept, not knowing where she was or why she was in that car, taken from her home and her parents. She didn't hear the car stop and the woman ordered out and into a forested area. She didn't hear the woman's pleas for mercy or the shot that reverberated through the forest, ending the cries and sobs.

The man stood for a moment, staring down at the body, before he turned and walked away, not caring that she wasn't buried. He would never know that hunters found her the next day and that the authorities would spend years trying to identify her.

He slid behind the wheel of the car, not paying any attention to the little girl behind him, intent on reaching his destination. Three days later, he pulled to a stop near a police department, hesitating on for a few seconds, before he yanked open the car door, pulled the little girl from her seat, and sticking an envelope into her coat. Looking around, he walked to the steps of the department and set her down between the doors, not seeing anyone at the front desk. He turned, walked back to his car and drove away, not looking back, not caring that he had disrupted lives. He would stay in the area and make sure his plans were followed, that was a given.

A police officer returning to the front desk hesitated as he heard sobs and catching movement at the front doors moved quickly that way, picking up the little girl and comforting her as best he could. He pulled out the letter and handed it to his sergeant.

They tried to find her parents but couldn't. They never did determine how she got there, turning instead to the foster care system for her. Years would go by and every once in a while the file would be opened and then closed, no closer to a resolution.

The little girl sobbed for her parents for days, finally settling down in her foster parents' home, but knowing inside her she was missing people important to her.

Chapter 1

$\mathcal{D}$ucking his head to see out the pass-through window from the kitchen of his cafe, The House, Joshua Smithson stared across the floor and out the large front window, one Amy, his head server, was working to decorate for Christmas. It was the last few days of November and the first of December was a big day in the town of Mistletoe. He shook his head at his thoughts. This year, he just wasn't in the mood for Christmas. His eyes dropped to the food he was preparing and then shot back up as he heard Amy yell and then three or four men in the cafe run for the door, yanking it open before they hit the sidewalk, heading across the street.

"Amy? What on earth?" Josh dropped the knife he held in his hand and headed for the door.

Amy was standing there, shaking. "Someone just ran up on the sidewalk. I'm not sure what's going on. It looks as if they were cut off." Her hands covered her mouth as she stared out, fear for the pedestrians in her mind.

"Stay here with the other ladies and children. I'll be right back."

Josh stood for a moment, his eyes searching the area, feeling something off but not quite sure what it was. He finally shook his head and headed back to his cafe, the food not cooking itself, he thought.

"Josh?" Amy quiet voice came to him as he stood for a moment, lost in thought.

"Yeah, Amy?" He looked up, his face clearing of his thoughts, black as they could be at times.

"What happened out there?"

Josh shrugged. "I have no idea. Mrs. White said she was cut off by someone, who hit the front fender of her car and sent her towards the sidewalk. Thank God, no one was hurt."

Amy shuddered. "It could have been so much worse. Still, there had to be a reason for this. Things like this don't just happen in Mistletoe. At least, they didn't until you and your friends moved here." She smirked at him as she walked away.

Josh gave a shout of laughter, then stopped in his movements as he heard the soft click of the back door. He dropped his head enough to look out front again. No, he had everyone who was scheduled to work out there and the students who worked the kitchen were with him. So, who had just entered? He turned slowly, his eyes searching, stopping when he saw the young woman standing there, her eyes on the floor, shaking and not just from cold, he thought.

He walked slowly towards her, finding her shrinking back from him. He stopped, a hand going out, as he murmured soft words, words he didn't even know he was uttering. She finally reached a tentative hand out to his. Your hand's ice cold, girl, and not just from the weather. You're frightened of something, Josh thought, his heart automatically sending up a prayer. No, he amended his thoughts. No frightened. Terrified is more like it.

"Are you okay?" When she didn't respond he sighed. Now what?

"Josh?" Amy's voice came from behind him. "Who's this?" She stopped short as he raised his free hand.

"I don't yet, Amy. She's not looking at me or talking. I'm going to try and talk her into sitting in my office. Can you call Tom for me? I think we need the police here for this."

The woman's hand jerked back as Josh's words and she stepped backwards, stopping when she hit the wall behind her, her shaking increasing. Josh frowned. Whatever was going on, she needed help and needed it now.

"Amy, can you find Old Jack or Blackie for me? I need one of them for their medic experience." Josh knew both men had served in the armed forces as medics, Blackie one of his good friends. He finally reached and gently grasped the woman's arm, trying to turn her towards the hallway that led to his office, but she pulled free and ran for the door, shoving it open and running through it, Josh on her heels.

He caught up to her, surrounding her with his arms even as she struggled with him, her hand catching his cheek, leaving it smarting. Josh sighed to himself. This was not how I planned my day, Lord. Why me? Then the thought changed. I know, Lord, I know. Why not me?

He looked over his shoulder at his restaurant, knowing he was never going to get the lady back inside there. He reached for his keys, clicking the fob to unlock the doors and pulling open the passenger door on his SUV. He gently tucked her inside, waiting for her to do up her seatbelt. She sat, her eyes finally raised to his face, clear gray eyes that held terror and something else he couldn't place. He pulled out the seatbelt, reaching across her to fasten it, feeling her shrink back from him.

Shutting the door and locking it, he stood for a moment, his eyes on her through the window, seeing she had lowered her face again. He turned, keys still in hand, to walk around the back of his vehicle, hearing the whisper of a sound and raising his arm enough to ward off the bat heading for his head. His arm dropped, numb in feeling, and he wasn't even sure that it hadn't been broken. He dodged as he saw the bat heading his way again, hearing it strike the vehicle. He raised his head enough to get a glimpse of the man, tall, overweight, hat pulled down enough to shade the upper portion of his face, scarf wrapped around the bottom of the face. Well, that's that, he thought. The bat raised again, the man hesitated, his head turning before he ran away from Josh, heading towards the centre of the town, the bat swinging from his hand.

Josh leaned back again his vehicle, his breathing ragged, his arm supported by his other hand. He turned to look back into the vehicle. She was still there, her face white as she stared back at him, fear flowing from her.

Josh moved to walk back around, but hands on his arm stopped him.

"Josh?" His friend, Levi Blackwell, stood there, concern colouring his face.

"I'm okay, Blackie. The arm? I'm not too sure about."

"Let me take a look at it." Blackie's hands reached to feel the arm, stopping when Josh shook his head.

"Not right now. Grab my jacket from the cafe and follow me home, will you? I have a lady in the car that I need you to assess for me."

For the first time, Blackie realized that Josh wasn't on his own. "A lady? Who is she?"

"I have no idea. I hadn't gotten as far as introductions yet. Maybe…". His voice died away. "Is Julia free?"

"She'll make herself free." Blackie ran for the back door, meeting Amy standing outside the back door with Josh's coat in her hands and having a few words with her.

"Here. You're not going to get that on, though."

Josh grabbed his jacket and dumped it into the back seat. "I won't even try. See you in a few."

Blackie stood, watching as his friend drove away, concern on his face before he turned, heading for his office and his wife. Julia would definitely be needed.

    *S*he stood in Josh's kitchen, afraid to look around, afraid to look up, not knowing what was going on. Her head was pounding and making it difficult for her to think clearly, and she needed to do that. She felt gentle hands helping her out of her jacket and then on her arms, leading her to a chair when she was gently shoved down, and the man knelt to remove her boots, rising to set them near his on the boot tray.

    She listened to water running, then the beep of a microwave before a cup of peppermint tea was set in front of her. She couldn't make her hands reach for it and then his hands came into her line of sight, reaching for hers and wrapping them around the cup.

    She listened to his steps moving away and then whispering back across the floor behind her. She jumped as she felt his hands on her shoulders and realized he was tucking a warm blanket around her. He didn't speak, just was there if she needed anything.

Josh watched her from where he was setting coffee to perk. He shook his head. What had God just led him into, he wondered? And was he ready for it? He rubbed at his arm, feeling the pain. Not broken, he thought, but bruised.

He walked towards the front door as he heard a light tap and then the door opening, hugging Julia, Blackie's wife, before he nodded to the kitchen. Julia headed that way, an exclamation coming from her.

Blackie's hand on his arm kept him in place.

"Josh? What's going on? You didn't explain earlier."

Josh shrugged. "I'm not really sure, Blackie. She ended up in my cafe kitchen. She needs medical aid but I don't think I'll get her to the hospital. That's why I asked for you to come, you or Old Jack. She's not saying anything at all but she's terrified. I can see that."

He looked up as Julia came towards them, a troubled look on her face.

"Blackie, I have a bag in the back of the truck. The one from Emily's. I need it. I've talked our friend into a shower and there's some clothes in there I think will pretty much fit her."

Blackie reached to kiss his wife before he turned to head back outside.

"Josh? Your spare room is ready, isn't it?"

He nodded. "It is. There are towels in the cupboard just outside it if you want to change them, but I just put fresh ones in the bathroom yesterday. There is shampoo and what not that Joy left under the sink." He looked towards the kitchen even as his thoughts went to his sister, who was due to visit in a day or two. "How is she?"

"She's not talking. I don't like that. Let me get her into the shower and changed and then see what we can do. I'll have Blackie check her out then for us."

Josh paced his kitchen, his heart lifted in prayer, even as he waited for the women to return. Blackie heard Julia's soft call and walked towards her, staying for a few minutes before he returned, a troubled look on his face, the women following after him.

Josh stood for a moment, his eyes on the lady as she sat once more in the chair, before he approached and crouched down in front of her. He winced as he saw the bruising and cuts on her face. His gaze shot to Blackie, who nodded.

"There's one on her temple that concerns me. We need to get her in and get it checked out but she's refusing to go." He looked around. "I called Doc. He's agreed to come over in a bit."

Josh nodded, his dark brown eyes back on her gray ones. Her dark red hair was still wet from the shower but he could see the curls in it.

"Can you talk to me? Tell me your name?"

He could see her hesitating and wasn't quite sure why. He barely heard her response.

"Leah. My name is Leah."

"That's good, Leah. Do you have a last name? Most of us do." Josh gave a quick grin as Julia slapped him lightly on the shoulder as she walked past him, bringing Leah's eyes to him and then to her, fear briefly making an appearance.

"I don't remember." Tears gathered, making her eyes dark murky pools. "Why can't I remember?"

Josh reached for her hands. "It's okay, Leah. It will come back to you. I have a friend, a doctor. He's going to come and talk to you." He saw her look of fright. "It's okay. He's not going to hurt you. I just want him to check you over and make sure you're okay. Blackie here was a medic in the armed forces but isn't in that field any more."

She finally nodded. "I don't remember what happened. I just remember someone walking towards me in a building and I froze and ran." She looked at him, seeing his nod. "That was you, wasn't it?" She snatched her hands back, bringing them to her mouth. "He went after you. Did he hurt you?"

Josh shrugged off her concern. "Nothing broken. Just a bruise. But why would he be after you?"

"But who was he? And why was he after me?" Her fright was palpable as she stared at him, then raised her eyes to study Blackie and Julia.

"We don't know that. Yet." Blackie spoke up. "Josh said you ran when he mentioned the police. Any reason why?"

She shook her head. "I have no idea. I'm sorry." She looked up at the three of them, distress and something else they couldn't read in her eyes. "I just don't remember."

Josh stood and moved to the kitchen doorway as he heard the front door open and close, giving a quiet hello to Simon Gardner, another friend.

Simon dropped his coat on a chair in the living room, kicked off his boots, and moved to the kitchen, his socked feet quiet on the floor, greeting his two other friends, taking a look at Leah, and then reaching for the coffee pot. He had dropped in on his way home from work as a police officer, his badge and weapon still on his belt. He spun as he heard the stifled scream from Leah, coffee spilling across his hand and he grimaced, reaching for a wet cloth to wipe it off.

Leah's jump had shoved her chair back hard enough that it toppled over as she moved way from Simon, her hands to her mouth. They could feel the fear coming from her but didn't understand why.

She stopped as she ran into Josh, whose arms encircled her from behind. She struggled against his grasp, finally hearing the soothing words he was murmuring and her fight stopped as she leaned back against him.

Simon's startled eyes sought Josh before a frown came over his face. He had a good memory for faces and something about the lady Josh was holding seemed familiar.

"Leah? Are you okay now? Simon is a good friend of ours. He will not hurt you in any way. Do you understand?" Josh's words were quiet in her ear, his blond hair so close to her own head making a sharp contrast.

She finally nodded, letting him release her, her hand swiping at the tears on her cheeks.

"I'm sorry. I have no idea why I'm scared of the police."

Simon nodded. "It's understandable. Josh let me know what was up when he called earlier. I gather you don't remember your full name?"

She shook her head even as she heard Josh righting her chair and gently shoving her down into it again. "I don't. I have no idea. And I'm not even sure Leah is my correct name." She looked around at them. "How do I find out?"

"First, we can take your picture and run it through our system, to see if there are any warrants, etc, out for you. Fingerprints too." Simon held up a hand as Josh went to protest. "I know, Josh. It sounds as if I'm treating her as a criminal, but I'm not. Then we check for missing persons reports that would match you."

Josh walked Simon out to his car later, deep in conversation with his friend.

"What now, Simon? How do we keep her safe if we don't know who she is or who she's running from?"

"You're sure she's running?" Simon shot a quick look at the house before turning to his friend again.

Josh nodded. "I'm sure. The fear that came from her after the attack was real. I didn't see enough of the man to get a good description. That's frustrating."

"It is. We'll work with what you've given Tom and see where we go. Stay safe."

Josh stood for a moment, his face turned to the clear night sky, the stars twinkling white against the blackness. He started as he heard a voice beside him.

He spun, startled to see Old Jack, a well-known figure in town, standing beside him.

"Just where did you come from?" Josh demanded.

"I've been waiting out here for a while. Knew you'd come out sooner or later. That lady you have in there?" He nodded towards the house.

"What about her?" Josh demanded. "Do you know her?"

Old Jack shook his head. "No, I don't. Not really. Saw her around town for the first time yesterday. She holed up in one of the abandoned buildings near your cafe last night. Word on the street is that she's running from someone, only no one knows who. If your friend there looks outside of town, he'll likely find her car off the road somewhere."

Josh nodded. "I'll give him a call." He turned to the house for a moment, then turned back to see Old Jack walking away from him. He sighed, frustrated that the older man had just left like that.

"Was that Old Jack?" Blackie stopped on the porch, watching as Josh walked towards him.

"It was. I guess Leah hit town yesterday at some point. He saw her. He thinks her car is outside of town somewhere, wrecked."

"That makes sense. The nicks on her face could have come from flying glass." Blackie stood for a moment, his hands jammed into his pockets, shoulders hunched against the cold. "Where is she spending the night? She can't stay here with you."

Josh sighed. "I know. I have no idea. Unless…". Josh backed away, taking a look at the detached garage. "She could use the apartment there."

Blackie shook his head. "That won't work. People will still talk, Josh, and we can't have that." He turned as Josh walked up the steps. "Julia and I can stay here tonight and then we can figure something out in the morning. Right now, this is where Leah feels safest. We don't want to change that on her."

Chapter 3

*H*ands running through his hair, Josh stared at Leah in frustration, not liking that she wanted to walk away from the town or walk away from him. He didn't want that for her. He wanted to find out why she was so scared and of whom. Please don't let her leave me, Lord, he prayed, not quite sure what all he meant.

"I have to, Josh. If someone is really after me, they'll go after you too." Leah was terrified of just that, without knowing exactly why.

"I can handle them, Leah. It's you I'm worried about." He pointed to the kitchen. "Come on out here and sit. You didn't even have your breakfast yet and you need that."

She finally brushed past him and dropped into a chair, not happy with him, but knowing he was right. She needed to eat. She just didn't want to be there. But where she wanted to be, she didn't know either.

Josh stared at her for a moment, then shook his head as he followed her, watching as Julia turned from the counter to speak to her. He froze, his eyes shooting between the two women before he spun and headed for his office. Blackie had been standing watching Josh and Leah and now followed his friend to his office.

"Josh?" Blackie's question had Josh putting up his finger in a wait motion.

Josh searched the internet, putting in Leah's first name and Julia's maiden name, before he sat back, sighing in relief but troubled as well.

"I know Leah's last name, Blackie."

"You do? And just how do you know that?"

Josh beckoned Blackie around to where he could see the computer monitor. Blackie stopped, frozen in place for a moment.

"She's related to Julia and that means Finn as well. How'd you know?"

"When Julia turned in there, there was a similarity. I wasn't sure until I checked." He reached to draw up his email program, sending off a quick message to Simon and then to Blackie's father, Samuel. "I'll get your Dad to look into her and see what he can find." He spun in his chair, his eyes on the door. "How do I tell her?"

"Tell me what?" Josh drew a deep breath as he saw the two ladies standing there.

He rose and walked towards Leah, catching her hand and drawing her across to his desk chair. "Sit for a moment. I found out who you are."

"You did? How?"

Josh nodded towards Julia at her question. "You looked like Julia there for a moment when she turned." His eyes raised as he heard a sound from Julia and saw that she had her hands to her mouth even as Blackie had his arm around her.

"She looks like Finn, Josh. Blackie. Why didn't I see that last night?"

"Because we were too concerned about how she was feeling. I think we did see it, we just didn't recognize it." Josh perched on the corner of his desk, reaching to turn the chair slightly so that Leah could see the monitor. "This is you. I've asked a friend to research you." He held up a hand as she went to protest. "No, it's Blackie's father. He will not tell anyone at all, not unless you agree to it. I also sent your name to Simon. He needs to know. Again, he will be very careful as he searches for whoever may be after you."

She finally nodded, her eyes still on his face, not on the monitor. She started as he pointed at the screen and she finally turned, her hand reaching out to touch her face on the screen.

"Leah Bronagh. That doesn't sound familiar, but that is me. Could I have been using another name?"

"That's what we'll find out." Josh shared a look with Blackie, knowing the fight had just begun and once again they had no idea who they faced or what it would all involve. He grew fearful, knowing that Leah was in danger and he didn't like that, not one bit. Lord, protect my lady, he prayed, without being conscious of how he had prayed.

Blackie excused himself as his phone rang and he walked away to answer, standing where he could see both Josh and Leah. Simon was on the other end, having receiving Josh's email and wanting more information. Blackie finally pocketed his phone, walking back towards the other three, his eyes on Leah.

"Josh, Simon's confirmed Leah's identity. He also say that an abandoned car was found just outside of town. Someone did a number on it, he said, likely with a bat."

Josh rose to his full height. "A bat? Like our friend from last night?"

Blackie nodded. "That's what he's thinking. Old Jack was right, you know. How does he know these things?"

"I asked him one time." Julia's voice was quiet. "He says God talks to him and tells him things."

"I suspect that is what happens." Blackie looked at Leah, seeing once more the fear on her face. "We'll keep you as safe as we can, Leah. That's a promise." He wrapped an arm around his wife. "Julia and I had an adventure ourselves as did another couple, Jacob and Finn." He looked at Josh, seeing his nod. "Now, I suggest we take you to Finn's parents. They have a B&B and I know they'll put you up."

"I can't." Leah was almost in tears. "I can't put anyone else in danger." She turned to Josh, her eyes beseeching him to let her stay.

"We'll talk about it, okay, Leah? My sister's due in sometime today. That would work if you stay here."

Blackie tilted his head towards the living room and Josh hesitated, his eyes on Leah. He felt Julia's hand on his arm and looked down at her, nodding as she motioned him to follow Blackie.

Julia turned to Leah, wondering how they were related after all.

"Josh, just what are you thinking?" Blackie had a good idea of his friend's thoughts, having served in the armed forces with him for eight years.

Josh shrugged as he paced his living room, hands jammed into his jeans' pockets. "I don't know, Blackie. I really don't know. I just can't let her walk away from me. You know that."

"I know. It was like that for Julia with me." Blackie sighed. "Is Joy coming in on her own or are Jeremiah and the girls with her?"

"She didn't say, but I suspect that Jeremiah will be with her. He did say the church here had asked him to fill in for the pastor while he's on sabbatical. I never heard what his answer was."

Blackie nodded. "That would make sense. If they're here, Leah would be able to stay. You know how small towns are. If they're not here, you'll have to find somewhere for her to stay."

Josh nodded, a troubled look on his face. "I know and I have no idea where that would be. She won't go to Finn's people, I know that."

Blackie shot a look at Josh before turning to where Julia stood in the office doorway. "Let us know what you decide. We have to run. Don't do anything abruptly."

Josh shook his head. "I don't think I'd get away with that." He grinned for a moment as Julia shook a finger at him. "I'll watch out for your cousin or whoever she is, Julia."

Josh stood for a moment, his eyes following Blackie and Julia as they walked out the front door, his mind racing as to where Leah could stay. He finally turned back to the office, knowing he needed to head for his cafe, but hesitant to take her with him. His phone ringing stopped him in his tracks.

Amy was on the line, letting him know she had called in staff and he didn't really need to show up today. They had it covered. He thanked her, knowing the cafe was in good hands, and that he had a day to make plans. Or rather, a day to find out God's plans.

Leah looked up at him, a frown on her face.

"It doesn't make sense, Josh. Why don't I remember?"

"That happens. Remember what Doc said. Sometimes we block things that are so traumatic we can't deal with them at the time." Doc had dropped by the night before, looked Leah over and basically told them she was fine, that she had a concussion but was blocking something and he had no idea what, or when her memory would return.

"Now what, Josh? I can't keep you from your work." Leah shoved herself from his chair and paced, heading for the living room, fatigue suddenly overcoming her.

"I don't have to be there today, Amy called. She's arranged for staff to come in for me. We're good that way." He watched as she stumbled slightly in her walk, seeing the deep-rooted fatigue and knowing it wasn't just from the last few days. "Here, sit on the couch. You're going to fall down if you don't."

She finally nodded, sinking down on the soft material of the couch and then stretching out. "Don't let me sleep, please, Josh. I can't handle the dreams if I do." Her eyes closed, her breath evened out and she was asleep.

He watched for a moment before heading for the bedroom she had used and snagging one of her pillows. He tucked it under her head and then reached for the soft blue blanket that one of his nieces had left the last time his sister was in town. He tucked it over her, brushing back the hair from her face, wincing at the dressing Doc had placed on her temple. She was hurting in more ways than one, he thought, and he had no idea how to help her. Silent prayers rose from his heart. What were the dreams she can't handle, Lord? Grant her a peaceful sleep this day.

Josh raised his head mid-afternoon, his finger marking his place in his Bible. He had wandered the house, caught up on his office paperwork, answered all the emails he had waiting, searched the internet for more information on Leah, and then reached for his Bible, turning to his favourite book of Joshua. He needed to be reminded that he had to be strong, to have courage, that God was in control. His eyes sought Leah, seeing she was still sleeping, and glad for that. He rose, setting his Bible down and hearing for the door as it opened and feeling a rush of cold air that entered. He shivered for a moment as he stood, watching his sister as she carefully shut the door and then shrugged out of her coat and boots before she turned, seeing him standing there.

Joy Williams reached for her brother, drawing him into a tight hug. Something was going on with him, she just knew, she just didn't know what. Both she and her husband, Jeremiah, had felt the need to be there, that Josh needed them. They had planned the trip anyway but made it two days earlier than planned. Somehow Josh had known that.

She stood back, her eyes on her brother, younger by ten minutes, seeing the fatigue and stress there.

"Josh?"

He lifted a finger to hush her and then nodded to the kitchen. "There's hot water on the stove. I just boiled it." He looked at his watch. "Scratch that. We'll need to heat it. That was some hours ago I did that."

Joy shook her head at him as she walked past him, seeing the disarray in his kitchen and knowing that wasn't him. She moved to clean it, Josh leaning a shoulder against the door frame as he watched, their conversation quiet, picking up with they had left off months ago. It was like that for the twins.

"Where're Jeremiah and the girls?"

"Outside. They were fascinated with the snow you have here. We don't have any. He's letting them run off energy." She turned, her cup of tea in her hand. "What's going on, Josh? I know something is."

Josh studied her for a moment, before he shot a look over his shoulder, and then stared at the floor. He wasn't quite sure how to respond to that, not when he really didn't know himself. He turned as he heard the door open, and a man's quiet voice admonishing his daughters to be quiet, that Uncle Josh might be sleeping. He was up early, he reminded them.

Josh grinned at the exaggerated steps the two little girls were taking as they walked towards the kitchen, trying hard to be quiet, before they saw him and raced towards him, confident in his greeting. He dropped to the floor, arms reaching out to hug the two little ones, taking the hugs and kisses they showered him with.

"Uncle Josh! You're not sleeping!" Three-year-old Heidi was thrilled. "Daddy said you were." She threw a dark look at her father.

"Not today, sweetheart. I didn't have to work, so I'm already rested. How come you're here?"

"It's a surprise." She looked up at her mother. "Can we tell Uncle Josh?"

Her mother nodded, even as two-year-old Holly reached hands to her uncle's face, turning it towards him.

"Unca Osh. Can you play with us?"

"It's Uncle Josh." The superior tone in Heidi's voice had Josh's body shaking with suppressed laughter even as he heard the parents laughing out loud.

"What I said. Unca Osh."

Heidi slapped her forehead in despair, a movement that had become common for her in the last few months. Where it came from, no one was quite sure.

"It's okay, Heidi. I'll answer to either one." He hugged the two girls before he set them down and rose, his hands on their heads. "What brings you to town so early?"

Joy shared a look with Jeremiah, even as he walked past her to reach for the coffee pot and pour both himself and Josh a cup. It was home, Josh's house, to them.

"It's like this, Josh." Joy's voice held worry for a moment. "Jeremiah's taking over as interim pastor for yours for now. And Blackie has asked if he'd consider counselling at his youth centre. We've prayed about this long and hard, and here we are."

Josh had listened, happiness growing inside him, knowing his beloved sister and her family would be moving to his town. He reached to hug her, and then Jeremiah, the two little ones demanding their share. As the adults settled down in the kitchen, Heidi crawled up on her mother's knee. Holly headed for the living room, knowing her uncle had books there on the shelf for her.

Chapter 4

*S*ensing she wasn't alone any more, Leah slowly awoke, her eyes flickering open and closed, until they finally stayed open. She felt the pillow under her head, frowning as it hadn't been there when she fell asleep and then touching the blanket that covered her. She smiled slowly, warmth filling her as she realized Josh had made her comfortable, in herself knowing that she was almost a complete stranger to the comfort he had provided her. Scratch that. She was a complete stranger to it lately, she thought. Her eyes searched the room, not seeing him, but seeing his well-used Bible on the table by his chair. Well, Lord, it looks as if You led me to a Christian man. Now what? I can't stay here, that's a given.

She sat up, reaching to fold the blanket and set it neatly on the couch before pushing the hair back on her face. She sat, lost in thought, before she heard a small squeal and jumped, searching for the sound. She spotted the little girl, on her knees near the bookshelf, her eyes on her, a startled look on her face that changed to joy before the little one was on her feet, running towards her, a squeal of happiness coming from her.

"Leah - you here?   At my Unca Osh's?"   Holly threw herself into Leah's arms, her own arms tight around Leah's neck.

"I'm sorry. Do I know you?" Leah was hesitant to move, not sure what was going on.

Holly sat back, her hands still locked around Leah's neck as she nodded vigorously. "You do.   You teach me. At Sunnay."

"I do?"   She looked up, puzzled as Josh hit the room, almost on a run, not quite sure what was happening, Joy and Jeremiah on his heels, Heidi running past them, overjoyed to find a friend at her uncle's.

Josh slid to a stop, his eyes astonished as he watched Heidi throwing herself on Leah as well.

"I take it you know these two?"

"Apparently, I do. Unfortunately, I don't remember that I do." Her eyes held his for a moment, seeing understanding in his before they slid to Joy, who stood beside her brother, a hand on arm, surprise on her face.

"Leah MacLeod? What are you doing here, in Mistletoe and at my brother's at that?"

Leah shook her head. "I'm sorry. I really don't know." She looked down at the two little ones cuddling close to her before she looked back up. "You know me?"

Joy approached, sitting beside Heidi, her hand going out to touch Leah's shoulder. "We do. You're the girls' favourite Sunday school teacher. I don't know you as well as I would like to. But that doesn't explain why you're here." She turned as she heard a sound from Jeremiah, who watched Leah, a frown in place.

"Girls, I think I heard Uncle Josh say he had some new toys for you two upstairs in the playroom. Now would be a good time to find them." At their protest, their father held up a hand. "Now, please, girls. Leah will be here for a while. She won't leave without saying goodbye, but somehow, I don't think that's happening." He had caught a look on Josh's face that he had seen on others, and knew Josh had no intention of letting Leah escape from him, not if he could help it.

The two girls slid to the floor, reluctant to leave Leah's side, but obedient to their father's request. With one final glance backwards, they headed upstairs, quiet chatter flowing back to the adults.

Josh sat down across from Leah, his eyes on her, even as she studied first Joy and then Jeremiah. "Leah? Do you remember these people at all?"

She looked back at him, sadness in her face and her voice as she responded, her head shaking. "I don't, Josh. I'm sorry. The littlest one, I almost do, but it's so shadowy I can't be certain."

Josh sighed, knowing that she was correct. His eyes caught Joy's look at Leah, puzzlement on her face, even as he heard Jeremiah cross the floor and sit in a chair near the couch.

"Joy, you say you know Leah?"

"We do. From church. What, about two years now, Jeremiah?"

He nodded, a look on his face that made Josh want to question him. "About that."

"Your name's Leah MacLeod." Joy stopped at a sound from Josh and then saw Leah shaking her head. "Yes, that's what we know you as. It's not correct?" Her eyes flew to her husband's, seeing compassion and relief there. "Jeremiah?"

"That's the name she was going by, but it's not her real name. I couldn't say anything, Joy. You know that."

"I know. This is so hard." She turned to Josh. "What is her name then?"

"Leah Bronagh." All eyes turned to Leah as she spoke. "Josh figured it out this morning. A friend and his wife were here. Apparently I looked like Julia and he searched under my first name and her maiden name."

"Blackie's wife? They're related?" Joy's hands went to her mouth. "That means Finn as well. Josh, what did you just go and walk into?"

Josh laughed at the expression on his sister's face before he sobered. "We have no idea, Joy. Jeremiah, now that it's out in the open what Leah's name is, did she tell you anything that might help?"

Jeremiah's eyes sought Leah, who nodded, giving him permission to speak. "Not really. She just said she needed to hide from someone but wouldn't tell me who or why. That's all she said. She asked if she could be known by a different name, a relative's I think she said." He paused, not quite certain what was going on. "That doesn't explain how she ended up here, of all places."

Josh started to laugh even as Leah shook her head at him. "She wandered into The House yesterday, ran from me, I was attacked by a bat-wielding man who was after her, and then I brought her home."

Joy frowned. "That sounds like you brought home a stray dog, Josh."

The three others broke out into laughter, even as Leah agreed that was exactly what it sounded like. Jeremiah rose as he heard Heidi calling for him, returning with the girls in his arms, before settling down, his daughters cuddling down beside him. Leah watched them, seeing the love between father and daughters, and somehow knowing that had not been her lot.

Josh's head turned as he heard a tap at the door and then the door opening. Blackie and his father, Samuel, stood there, waiting to greet Joy and her family.

"Blackie. Samuel.   I take it you've found out something."

"We have. Dad wanted to talk to Leah in person, so we headed over here. Julia's still at the office.   Jacob needed her assistance on something." Julia worked in the office Blackie and another friend, Jacob, shared. Blackie walked forward to hug Joy and then reach to shake Jeremiah's hand, picking up Heidi who reached up for a beloved friend.

Samuel greeted the others, then sat, watching Leah, seeing movements that reminded him of his beloved daughter-in-law.   What now, Lord?   What have we walked into?

"Samuel?   You've found out something?" Josh's quiet voice broke into his thoughts.

Samuel turned to answer Josh, his eyes on Leah. "We have, Josh, and it's not at all what we expected.   Leah, you have remembered nothing?"

She shook her head. "I have flittering memories, but nothing that stays long enough for me to recognize or even see clearly. Why?"

Samuel sighed.   How did he even begin, Lord, he asked? "Leah, we've been able to track what we can of your life. You entered foster care at age 3, as to why, that we can't find out. You were raised in one foster home, a very loving one at that. They tried many times over the years to adopt you but each attempt was turned down. That, we can't find out why, but I'm still looking into it.

"You left there abruptly as soon as you turned eighteen, not because they asked you to.   You didn't give a reason, but they suspect you were scared of something or someone.   They have tried to get you to open up over the years but you wouldn't.

You broke contact with them about two years ago and haven't seen or talked to them since. They want you to contact them, when you're ready.

"Now, as to why you're running. We think we have an idea, but we're not sure. Your foster sister remembers you receiving a letter just before you were eighteen that she says seemed to terrify you. You wouldn't tell her what was in or who it was from, but she says you changed after that. You were always watching around you for someone."

Leah stared at him, not quite sure if what he was saying was true or not. She finally shook her head. "I'm sorry. I really don't remember. And I should, I know." Her eyes traced to Josh's and stayed there, seeing the concern and compassion there as well as something else she just couldn't read.

"I'm sorry. I just don't remember." She leaned forward, her face buried in her hands. They could barely hear her. "How much danger am I bringing here?"

"We don't know that you are." Blackie watched as her head shot up at his words and he held up a hand. "I know.

You're thinking of yesterday and the man with the bat. And then there's your car. Someone has come after you and we need to find out who."

She rose and began to pace, her arms wrapped around herself before she spun. "So, then, how do we do that?" Her eyes went to the little girls, who were fascinated with the conversation, even though they couldn't really understand what was being said. "I can't bring danger to those two."

Jeremiah nodded. "And we won't let you. We'll guard both them and you. If I feel they are in danger, Joy's parents will be here and will take them to safety."

She finally agreed, then turned and walked away. They heard the faint click of her door closing before they looked at each other.

"Now what, Samuel? How do we find out what is going on? She's not faking this, forgetting who she is." Joy watched her brother closely.

"I know she's not, but I have no idea how to reach her." Samuel watched as Josh finally rose and walked away, hands jammed into his pockets. His eyes held compassion as he exchanged a glance with his son. Josh's heart was involved, he thought. Please protect my friend, Lord. Bring this to a quick and safe ending.

$\mathcal{J}$osh stood in the centre of his office at The House, his eyes on Amy as she talked to him, but his thoughts on Leah who was in the kitchen with his prep staff.

"So, it looks as if we're in good shape for the rush later this week and for the weekend." Amy watched her boss and friend closely, seeing stress on his face she had never seen. "Josh?"

"Yeah, Amy?" He brought his mind back to her. "Was there something else?"

She shook her head. "No. I just wondered if everything was okay with you." She was older than him by ten years and looked on him as a younger brother.

"I really don't know, Amy. I'm trying to figure out what's going with Leah and that's not going well."

"We're praying for it, Bill and I. Let us know if we can help in any way."

She walked away, her voice already teasing the prep staff and he heard their laughing answers. He dropped into his chair, knowing he should be in the kitchen with them, but knowing he had paperwork to do and cheques to sign.

"Josh?" Leah's quiet voice raised his head an hour later.

"Leah? I'm sorry. I just got involved here." He stood and walked towards her, seeing something different in her face. "What's up?"

"Why does everyone always ask that? My foster mother always said the sky." She stopped, hands going to her mouth in surprise. "I remembered something."

"Yes, you did." Josh grinned at her. "Doc said you'd remember. Looks like he was right, after all. Just don't tell him that." He laughed at the expression on her face. "But you wanted something, didn't you?"

"I did. Do you have time to walk around downtown with me? I don't want to go on my own, but I think I need to. I was heading here for a reason. Maybe that would trigger something."

Josh shot a look at the clock and sighed. It was coming up to his busy time of the morning, but he couldn't say no to Leah.

Leah caught the look on his face and turned away. "It's okay. I know you don't have time."

"Leah. Wait." He watched as she stopped, shoulders slumping in defeat. "Can you give me an hour or two? Then the rush will be over and I can walk with you. It usually slows down for a couple of hours after the breakfast crowd leaves."

She finally nodded, not wanting him to see the tears on her face. She walked away, heading for the staff break room and dropped to the couch there. She looked around. Josh had taken care to provide well for his staff, she thought. She didn't see him stop just outside the door and watch her, his heart in his eyes, before he turned and headed for the kitchen and the rush he could hear already starting.

Amy stopped by him. "Is Leah okay?"

"I think so. She's in the staff room. Could you check on her in a few minutes?"

He reached for the next order that needed preparing, not seeing Amy's look or the look she shared with one of the other staff, before she headed for the staff room.

"Leah?" She sighed as Leah jumped at her voice. "I'm sorry. I didn't mean to startle you."

Leah gave a half laugh. "Everything does these days and I have no idea why." She swiped at the tears, stopping as she saw the warm wet cloth Amy held out for her. "Thank you." Her voice was barely audible.

Amy sank down beside her, her hand going to Leah's arm. "I know it's a strange time for you. A strange town. Strange people. And you don't have anything you remember to base your feelings or reactions on, do you?" She waited until Leah nodded. "Josh out there? He's one of the good guys. So are his friends, Simon, Jacob, and Blackie. Never hesitate to go to one of them or Finn or Julia. Now, what can I do to help you?"

Leah shrugged. "I have no idea, but thank you for caring."

Amy patted her arm and then stood. "Sitting here moping won't help. Come on out when you're ready and we'll put you to work."

Leah stared after her, wonder in her thoughts that these people would just open up to a stranger and take them in. But then, she didn't feel like this town was a strange town to her. She felt like she had come home and she had no idea why.

Josh tucked Leah's hand into his arm an hour later, when, as promised, he headed out with her to walk the downtown area. He could tell she was nervous, and he couldn't say that he blamed her. She was in a new town, didn't know hardly anyone, and had already come under attack before she even reached the city limits.

She looked around, interest on her face, at the decorations that had been placed and those workers finishing off the large tree in the centre of the town square. Her footsteps slowed and she pulled Josh to a stop with her. She could feel someone behind her, but she wasn't sure if it was a friend or a foe.

Josh watched her glancing around, seeing the fear lurking in her eyes, and pulled her off to the side.

"Leah? What's going on?" His own eyes searched the crowd, but he couldn't distinguish if someone was out there after Leah or not.

"I don't know. I just feel someone out there." She shuddered from fear, not willing to let him see how deeply she was affected.

Josh shot a glance around and then, taking her hand, drew her into an antiquities store. The lady at the counter looked up, waved and then went back to her customer. Leah protested as Josh pulled her with him into the owner's office.

"We can't come in here, Josh. This is employees only."

He grinned. "It's okay. This is Finn's place. We're allowed." He pointed to a chair and waited until she finally sank down, with a mutinous look still on her face. He perched on the corner of the desk, his foot swinging idly as he watched the door, knowing Finn would be along as soon as she could and that Jacob would be there as soon as she called him, likely bringing Blackie and Julia with him. That would be good, he thought. Maybe we can come up with a plan.

He rose as he heard light footsteps heading his way and greeted Finn, who then turned to face Leah, a gasp coming from her.

"Who is this, Josh? She looks like Julia and I." Her glance shot between Josh and Leah.

"This is Leah Bronagh. Did Julia talk to you?"

"Just briefly. So, this is Leah. Welcome to town. I'm Finnola, also known as Finn. Jacob and I are married." She paused as a frown appeared on Leah's face. "You haven't met Jacob yet, I gather. He's another good friend of Josh, Blackie and Simon. I know you've met Blackie's wife, Julia."

Leah finally nodded even as a frown appeared once more. "Forgive me. I can't remember much, even as to why I was coming here to Mistletoe. Who names a town Mistletoe, anyway?" She looked up in surprise as the two with her laughed.

Finn chortled in glee. "That's what no one has ever been able to figure out, but it really does draw in the crowds in December."

Leah nodded. "I would like to look around your store, if I may. It looks fascinating."

Finn jumped up from the chair she had been sitting in and grasped Leah's hand, pulling her to her feet. "Come on. It's quiet right now. Besides, my sister-in-law, Ann, is here and she'll handle things for me."

Josh trailed along behind the two ladies for a while before he stood near the front window, his eyes watching the crowds passing by. Something was off, but he just wasn't sure what. He turned as he felt a hand on his back. Finn stood there, a troubled look on her face.

"Josh? What's her story?"

He shrugged. "No one knows, Finn. She can't remember." He sighed. "Apparently Joy and Jeremiah know her. She's taught the girls in Sunday school. But even Jeremiah doesn't know much. She just never shared." He glanced around, seeing

Leah standing talking with Ann. "Someone is after her, Finn, and I don't know who. I want to stop that, get her memory back, and then see what happens."

Finn smiled. "Your heart's involved, isn't it, Josh?" She waited until he gave a reluctant nod. "And you can't say or do anything until you know she's free. We'll pray for you both."

Josh dropped a kiss on Finn's cheek. "Thank you. That is appreciated." He turned as he saw Leah approaching him. "Ready to go?"

"I am." She thanked Finn and then headed for the door, Josh reaching it ahead of her, grinning at her protest that she could open her own door.

Finn watched them walk away, Ann at her side.

"They make a great couple, Finn. What's her story?"

Finn shrugged. "Right now, she doesn't even know. She was injured a few days ago and can't remember."

"Oh, no. And Josh has lost his heart. I can see that." Ann turned to Finn. "Now what, Finn, other than praying for them?"

"That's about all we can do, Ann." Finn watched the couple until they were lost from sight, a heaviness weighing her down.

Chapter 6

Glancing around, Leah shuddered in fear once more. Why, she had no idea, and she did not like that one bit. She wanted to remember but just couldn't. Maybe she should just leave town, but then, where would she go? She didn't know where she had come from. She had not asked that of Joy or Jeremiah. Not yet, anyway, but that would come, she knew.

Josh directed her to the town square and then past it, towards an area that held small buildings and decorated trees as well a a large gazebo. He stopped at a refreshment stand for teas for them and then pointed to the buildings.

"These are some of the older buildings from the original settlers, I think someone told me. They keep them closed all year but at Christmas they open them up for a few days. It's fascinating walking through them."

Leah stared at the buildings, a frown in place. "I know those buildings, Josh, but how?"

He stared at her for a moment, then sipped at his tea. "You know them? That's interesting. Come on. Let's walk closer to them."

Leah finally dumped her tea into a garbage bin, not really in the mood to drink it all. She stood watching the few people around them, a sense of doom overcoming her once more but she couldn't see anyone who threatened her. Josh watched her and then did his own watching of the crowds.

Turning as he heard his name called, Josh hesitated at leaving Leah but she urged him to go, that she would be all right. There were people around, weren't there?

Josh stood for some time speaking with Blackie until a loud snap and crashing broke shattered the air, as screams split through the sounds. Josh and Blackie spun, horror on their face as they saw one of the buildings had collapsed.

"Leah? Do you see her?" Josh's feet dug into the ground as he ran forward, not seeing her anywhere.

"The lady that was with me?" He slid to a stop near the older lady Leah had been talking to. "Do you know where she went?"

"No, I'm sorry. I think she went that way." A shaking finger pointed towards the collapsed building.

Josh's heart beat harder as he realized that Leah wasn't to be seen anywhere. He saw the man standing watching him and realized who was after Leah. He then heard cries that someone was trapped and knew it was Leah. His feet dug in once more as he started to run towards the building as Blackie tackled him, taking him to the ground.

"Let me go, Blackie. Leah's in there." Josh struggled against his friend's hold.

"We don't know that. The firemen are here. They'll check it out." Blackie's hold slipped on Josh and Josh was up and away, Blackie springing to his feet.

"Jacob!"   Blackie saw their friend watching the men working. "Stop Josh!"

Jacob raced towards Josh, taking him down, Blackie lending his weight to try and hold him to the ground. Josh fought them, struggling to get away, to reach the building. The two men's weight could barely keep him down and then Simon was there, aiding them.

Josh continued to struggle, almost getting away, his agonized eyes on the building, his body twisting and contorting under his friends as they tried to keep him still and safe.

"Let me up. I need to get to her." His cries reached his friends' ears but they still managed to keep him down. "Let me up. Please. Let me go."

Josh's struggles to escape almost succeeded until a team of paramedics arrived. Quickly assessing the situation and hearing his cries, they knew they had to restrain him.

"Who's he trying to get to?" The older paramedic was reaching into one of the boxes even as he asked even as the other paramedic lent his aid in an attempt to keep Josh on the ground.

"A friend.   We think she's in the building that collapsed."

"But they're closed.   She can't be." He shook his head at Blackie's comment.

Blackie drew in a ragged breath. "Josh thinks she is.   We can't see her anywhere." He shoved down on Josh's arm, just missing getting hit in the face. "Josh! Stop! We'll find her. You need to stop!"

Josh continued to fight against the men holding him, almost succeeding once more in getting free.   Blackie gave a grumble of concern, his hand reaching to pull the jacket and sweater sleeve back as he saw the syringe in the paramedic's hand, then struggled to hold Josh's arm still and to the ground, the tendons in the wrist corded and tight under his hand.   The second paramedic leaned on Josh's upper arm and even that was a struggle.   It took two of them to hold Josh's arm still enough for the injection to be given.

The paramedic sat back on his heels. "He's a fighter, isn't he? That's a sedative. It will knock him out for while.   We'll transport once he's no longer fighting us."

Blackie nodded as his eyes went back to his friend's face, seeing the agony there, the terror. He frowned as he heard Josh's voice whispering, the sound getting lower as the sedative took effect.

"I need to get to Leah. I need to find her. She's not safe. I know who's after her. Let me up." The last few words, or sobs rather, were barely audible as the sedative took effect and Josh lost consciousness, his body going limp, his head dropping to the ground.

His three friends shoved themselves away from him and rose, their eyes first on him, then each other.

"What did he just say?" Simon stared at Josh, and then at the collapsed building. "Does he really think she's in there?"

Blackie nodded. "He does. I don't see her." He spun in a circle, not seeing her, and then froze as he heard yells from the firemen at the collapsed building. "Simon?"

Simon nodded, his eyes on the Mistletoe Police Chief, Ed Waters, who stood watching them. "Ed?"

"Come on then, Simon. We'll check it out.   One of your friends is riding with Josh?"

Blackie nodded. "I will." He froze. "Joy!"

Jacob held up his phone. "Already on it.   Mary and your Mom are headed to Josh's. They'll watch the girls for Joy."

Blackie nodded. "I'll ride with him. Jacob?"

Jacob nodded. "I'll let the ladies know and then meet you there."

Simon walked away with the Chief, their conversation on Josh's words and the question that had been raised. Did he really know who was after Leah, and who was it then?

Chapter 7

Watching Josh walk towards Blackie, Leah stood for a moment, uncertain in what to do, frightened to be on her own, knowing someone was after her, but determined to stand on her own two feet. She finally turned and walked slowly towards the buildings, her eyes taking in the solidness of them, a wonder in her mind that buildings still stood after all those years, beaten by the weather to a soft gray. She stood for a moment, her eyes searching the area around her, before she walked towards one, stepping up on the small porch and approaching the window. She stood, hands cupped around her face as she stared inside.

Hearing a soft cry, she jumped back and looked around, a frown on her face. She heard the cry again, a mew, she thought, and searched for the kitten. Not finding it, she once more approached the window, looking inside and hearing the mew from inside the building. This is strange, she thought.

She tried the front door, finding it locked, more puzzled than ever. She stepped from the porch, searching for Josh and seeing him still talking with Blackie, his back turned towards her for a moment. She couldn't leave the kitten to go and get him. She walked around the building, searching for an entrance, stepping up on the back porch and heading for the door, hearing the mewing sounding louder. She tried the door, finding it unlocked, and hesitated, not knowing if she should enter or not. The cries of the kitten grabbed her attention once more and she slowly shoved the door open, stepping inside, determined to find the kitten and then get out before someone questioned why she was in a locked building.

She caught her breath at the beauty of the building in its simplicity. A school room, she thought. How I would have liked to have attended this school! She turned as she heard the cries and slowly walked forward, her eyes searching. She stopped as she heard a popping sound and then shrugged, moving forward. A second popping sound stilled her movements and she looked around, not quite sure what was going on.

The kitten's cries drew her forward as she searched for it, finally finding it crouched under a desk. She knelt and reached for it, cradling it close to her. As she stood, she heard a third popping sound, and looked up. The building seems to be moving, she thought, and turning, she began to walk rapidly towards the back door, the kitten cradled against her.

Snapping and cracking caught her attention, and this time she felt the building shudder. A low scream broke from her and she tried to run of the door, only to find beams and roofing falling in her way. She flung herself towards the wall, curling up in a ball, one hand over her head, the kitten tight in her other arm, praying for protection. Her head smacked against the old black iron stove, and she collapsed to the floor, darkness falling over her as the ringing in her head intensified. Josh, she thought. I need your help and I can't get to you.

Shouts rang broke through the air as the building slowly crumpled in on itself.

For a moment, everyone outside froze. Then men began to run towards the building, not sure what had happened. Sirens rang through the air as emergency personnel rushed to the scene, spilling from their vehicles, and heading for the buildings.

Calls went out, asking if anyone was inside. At first, the responses were negative, until one of the firefighters crouched down along the back wall and caught sight of Leah's jacket. Shouts for help rang through the air, catching the attention of the men with Josh, who were still fighting to keep him down and away from the building.

Working the men working carefully but quickly, the building was stabilized enough that the smallest of the firefighters, a younger woman, could slide inside and reach Leah. She quickly felt for a pulse, her heart thankful there was one. She felt Leah over, stopping as she saw the head wound. She frowned as she heard a mew and saw the tiny tip of an ear over Leah's arm. She tried to free the kitten, but Leah's hold was too strong. She turned at a question from outside, acknowledging that she needed the backboard and collar, and that she also needed help inside.

An paramedic joined her, glancing cautiously at the building as it still creaked and groaned, then helping to stabilize Leah before she was moved carefully to the opening and then outside.

The fire chief stood, eyes watchful, then disbelieving as he heard the kitten.

"She has a kitten in her arms?"

The young firefighter nodded. "She does, and she will not give it up. And we need her to do that. Her grip is too strong for me to release the cat."

Simon had moved closer and listened intently at the conversation going on around him, finally speaking.

"I know her. Maybe I can get the kitten from her." He moved towards Leah, his hand resting on her arm. "Leah. It's Simon. Can you let me have your kitten?" He waited, then moved his hand further on her arm to where the kitten was struggling to get free. "Come on, Leah. Let me have the kitten, please. I'll take care of it for you." He watched her face, then turned his attention to the little calico kitten, seeing her arm relax just a little.

He heard a whisper from her and bent close. "What did you say, Leah? Let me have the kitten, and then we'll get you some treatment for your head."

"The kitten was in the building. I had to get it. Josh needs it for the girls. I can't let it go." Her voice was barely audible and he could hear pain in it.

Simon gave a small smile, then finally managed to get the kitten from her. "It's okay, Leah. I'll take care of it for you. I'll make sure Josh gets it. Let them look after you now." He stepped back, unzipping his jacket enough to tuck the kitten in to keep it warm, his eyes on Leah's face, and his mind on her words.

Ed stopped beside him. "She went in after a kitten?"

"It appears that way. She wants it for Josh, she said. Why, I have no idea." He turned to look at the building. "But her going in there should not have brought the building down. They're monitored all the time for safety, particularly coming up to when the buildings will be opened for Christmas."

"I know. That concerns me. And who unlocked it, I would like to know." Ed walked away to speak with the fire chief as Simon turned to follow the stretcher bearing Leah.

Simon jumped up and took a seat, his eyes still on Leah, his thoughts puzzled as to what was going on with Josh and Leah. Now what, Lord, he asked. Only You know the outcome for this.

The paramedic looked askance as he saw the kitten peeking from Simon's jacket. "You know, they won't let the kitten in there."

"Ssh!" Simon grinned at him. "It's a therapy animal, isn't it? Leah wants Josh to have it for comfort. Isn't that what she said?"

The paramedic shook his head even as he grinned. "Not quite what I heard, but the intent was there. If you want to try it, it's your game. I'm staying out of it." He reached to adjust the IV, then assessed her pupils once more. "You said you know her?"

"Not well. She's just new to town. But she was injured somehow and lost her memory. Another concussion this close to that one won't help her any."

The paramedic looked up at him, then back at Leah. "No, it won't. But it may bring back her memory or drive it deeper. The docs will know best."

Simon waited until the stretcher was offloaded from the rig and then jumped down, his hand holding the kitten in place. He saw Julia heading his way and waited, greeting his friend.

"Where's Blackie?" Julie turned to enter the hospital, stopping as she heard a mew. "Simon?"

"I know. Leah rescued a kitten and I can't let it out of my sight." He grinned as she stared at him, finally shaking her head.

"I think you could." She looked around. "There's Ann. Let her have Leah's kitten and she'll take it over to Josh's."

The kitten quickly transferred hands, Ann agreeing to drop off the kitten, with a promise from them they would let her know how the two were.

Hours later, Joy stood in Josh's hospital room, watching as he moved restlessly, the sedative finally wearing off. Jeremiah's arm came around his wife.

"He's still not awake totally?"

Joy shook her head. "He's not. The doctor's not concerned though. He said they had to give him a lot and that with his fighting them at the time, it likely had an exaggerated effect. What have you heard about Leah?"

"She's in a room, still unconscious. They're concerned about her head injury, not knowing how it has affected her, on top of her previous one." He sighed. "I never expected this when we decided to move here."

"No, but I'm glad we're here." She took another look at her brother and then turned back to Jeremiah. "I need to go home to the girls." She groaned. "Did I just say home? Right now, we don't have a home."

"We do. Josh made that clear. Right now, we're where we need to be, just as you said." He kissed her, then helped her into her coat. "Go. Take care of the girls. I'll call if there's any change." He watched her walk away before he turned back to the bed, finding Josh's eyes flickering open and closed.

"Josh? Can you hear me, buddy?"

Josh finally focused on Jeremiah. "Jeremiah? Where am I?" His mouth and throat was dry and he had trouble getting his words out.

Jeremiah's hands went out to hold Josh's head up and the glass of water to his mouth, before he set the glass back on the table and reached to raise the head of the bed.

"You're in the hospital. Josh, do you remember anything?"

Josh went to shake his head, then stopped. "I can remember not seeing Leah. Where is she?"

"She's in another room here, Josh." Jeremiah paused, not quite sure how to continue.

"Is she okay?" Josh tried to push the covers back, but didn't have the strength. "Tell me."

"She's unconscious right now, Josh. And no, they will not let you in to see her. The chief has posted a guard at her door."

"A guard? Why?" Josh struggled to sit up, Jeremiah's hand on his chest preventing that.

"Someone sabotaged one of the buildings. She went in after a kitten and the building collapsed around her. They think she hit her head on the stove in the building and knocked herself out." He watched with compassion as Josh's head went back and his eyes slid closed.

"How does this affect her?"

"They don't know yet. They're waiting for her to wake up." Jeremiah paused, a smile lurking in his eyes. "Did you really want a kitten? I'm sure there were easier ways for Leah to get you one."

"A kitten? Who says I want a kitten?" Josh stared at Jeremiah, not quite sure if he was serious or not.

"Leah apparently does. She rescued a kitten and told Simon it was for you. That you needed it. For my girls. Shouldn't you have talked to me first?" He laughed at the expression on Josh's face. "Didn't know that, did you?"

Josh shook his head even as he yawned. "I don't remember us talking about animals at all. How do you know she said it was for me?"

"Simon. He had to talk her into giving it up. She told him it was for you." Jeremiah gave a small smile at the look that crossed Josh's face even as Josh lost his fight with sleep. He turned his head as he heard the door open and Simon walked in. "Where's Josh's kitten? He didn't know he needed one."

Simon gave a low laugh. "I hear tell your girls are fussing over it and Joy had to rescue it once again. What was she thinking, Leah, to go into a building?"

"None of us would have expected the building to collapse like that. It was planned, wasn't it?"

Simon nodded. "That's what we think. The fire chief has called in building inspectors and contractors to see what happened." He pointed with his chin towards Josh. "How is he?"

"Sleepy. He was awake just before you walked in. He tried hard to get up to go to Leah." Jeremiah paused, not quite sure how to proceed with what he needed to say.

"And you're concerned that his heart is already taken by her and you have no idea if she's free or not." Simon smiled in sympathy as Jeremiah finally nodded.

"That's it exactly. I heard how he fought you three. That's not him."

"No, it's not. But I can see him doing that for Joy and the girls."

Jeremiah nodded. "Yeah, I guess. Have you heard how Leah is? He asked."

"She was awake but not really doing much talking. I popped in to see her. She didn't recognize me, but the nurse says the doctors feel she's had another concussion and on top of one just days earlier, they are quite concerned. We'll have to talk about where she's to go when she's released." He nodded towards Josh. "He'll want to be close to her."

Jeremiah sighed. "I know he will. But how do we let him, when we don't know her history?" They both turned as they heard steps behind them. Blackie and his father, Samuel, stood there, greeting the two before Samuel moved to the side of the bed, his eyes on Josh who had just awakened again.

"Josh? How are you feeling?"

"A little groggy. What did they give me?"

Blackie moved closer, laughing at his friend. "A sedative, Josh. You were fighting us too hard to do anything else."

Josh finally nodded, his memory coming back. "Leah? Where is she?"

"She's here on your floor and no, you're not going to her." Samuel's hand rested on his young friend's arm. "I need to talk to you first." He glanced as the other three men. "It would be better if you all heard this now. That way, I don't have to repeat myself. The only missing is Jacob."

"And he's just outside. I heard his voice." Simon headed for the hallway, coming back with Jacob in tow. "Okay, Samuel. What did you find out?"

Chapter 8

*S*amuel's eyes studied the five younger men, lingering on Josh's face, knowing what he had to say would be disturbing but necessary. He sighed to himself, then prayed for wisdom in what he had to share. It should be shared with Leah first, but he wasn't able to, and he needed these men's help to keep her safe, if what he had uncovered was true.

"Dad?" Blackie's voice cut through his thoughts. "You have news?"

"I do, Levi. That I do, son. I'm not sure though how to explain it all so you understand." He held up a hand at their protest. "Just keep in mind that I should be talking with Leah first, and I just can't do that, not given her medical issues at present. I will as soon as the doctor gives me clearance." He studied each one, his eyes lingering on Josh the longest, knowing what he had to say would affect him the most.

Dad?" Blackie's voice once more caught Samuel's attention.

"Sorry, son. Okay. So, I guess I should start." He still hesitated, not quite sure what to say, and that was so unlike him. He prayed again for wisdom and words, and knew then that God was with him.

"Josh, you figured out your lady's name. She really is Leah Bronagh, one of the descendants from this town. That also makes her related to Finn and Julia. This is where her story becomes complicated and I'm still not sure how far back it goes, whether it goes back past her parents or not."

"What do you mean, Samuel?" Josh's eyes were stead on his friend.

"Her parents disappeared when she was three. We cannot track what happened to them. We cannot even prove that they are alive or dead. She was found on her own, a note pinned to her, giving her name, date of birth. Someone dropped her off at a police station. I know you've talked with her about how she was never adopted, although her foster family tried their best. There was some sort of documentation with her that she could never be adopted, something to do with her last name.

"There was no issues with her until just before she was 18. I talked to her foster family. The mother indicates something changed a couple of months before she was 18. Her foster sister said the same thing. She thought she had been contacted by someone, someone who terrified her. I have not been able to confirm this. We are looking into going to her apartment in your town, Jeremiah. We're just waiting for the police there to obtain a search warrant for us."

Jeremiah spoke up. "I have her permission from before to go into her place at any time for any reasons. She put it into writing and had a lawyer draw it up. So we can do that tomorrow if you like."

"That will help. Thank you."

"This seems to odd, Samuel." Jacob was trying to puzzle through it all. "Why couldn't she be adopted?"

Samuel shrugged. "That I have no idea why. From what I understand the documentation never said. Her foster parents have a copy and are emailing to me. I'll have it later today and maybe know something more."

Josh had been still, listening to them. "Donald Emms, from this town. How is he connected to the Bronaghs?"

The five men shared a look and then stared at him.

"Why would you ask that?" Blackie had his own issues with Donald, wanting to talk with him about a search he had sent Julia and Blackie on a year ago.

"Because he was standing watching Leah. I saw him when I turned to look for her at one point but I didn't recognize him right away.   He disappeared after the building collapsed." Josh's head went back and his eyes closed. "Why would he do this?"

"We don't know that he did, Josh." Simon spoke up. "But we will find out, trust me on that one." He glanced at his watch. "Sorry, Samuel. I'll have to catch up with you later. Let me know if I can do anything to help."

Samuel watched Simon walk away, knowing that Simon would never let this rest, not when it affected a good friend. He prayed for answers, that they could resolve this soon, without either Josh or Leah being hurt again.

"Samuel?" Josh's voice caught his attention. "Can you look into Donald? See where he is in this? I know Blackie wants to talk to him, but so do I. He knows something."

"I plan on doing just that."

The conversation had exhausted Josh, whose eyes slid closed as he slept again. The other men finished their quiet conversation and all left but Jeremiah.

Jeremiah stood for a few minutes at the window, his eyes on the sky, his heart raised in prayer. Sunday was only a few days away and he knew he needed to be working on his sermon, but right now, Josh needed him. He turned, leaning back against the wall, his hands jammed into his pockets, lost in thought before he walked out of Josh's room and down to Leah's. He nodded at the officer at the door and quietly pushed the door open.

Standing beside Leah's bed, he watched as her head turned restlessly before he reached to lay a hand on her shoulder and bow his head to pray for her. He looked up, surprised to see her eyes open and clear. The doctors didn't think she would be awake until the next day.

"Jeremiah? What are you doing here? And just where is here?" She looked around, panic momentarily taking over.

"You're in the hospital in Mistletoe. Don't you remember?"

She stared at him. "Mistletoe? Where's that? And why am I there?"

"You really don't remember?" When she shook her head, he sighed. Thanks, Lord, leaving it to me to break it to her. "You ended up here a few days ago. You couldn't remember anything other than your first name. Apparently you had an accident or something like that. Earlier today, you were in a building that collapsed here in town. They think you hit your head on an old cast-iron stove."

"Why would I be in that building? And why did it collapse?" She paused, a frown in place. "Jeremiah, this does not make sense at all."

"No, I guess it wouldn't." He reached to draw up a chair, knowing he'd be there for a while. "Mistletoe is where Josh lives."

"Joy's brother? But that doesn't explain why you're here."

"We're here because I'm taking over for the pastor for a while. He's off on sick leave. We're staying with Josh. Somehow you and Josh connected. You really don't remember?"

She went to shake her head, then stopped. "Does he have a restaurant or something?"

"He does. Why?"

"Then I do remember. He saved me from someone coming after me with a bat. He was hurt." Her eyes flew to Jeremiah's. "Tell me he didn't get hurt again."

Jeremiah began to laugh, drawing a frown from her. "No. He didn't get hurt again, but they did have to sedate him when he realized you were in the collapsed building. Blackie said he's never seen him fight to get to anyone like he found his friends."

She sighed, her head going back on the pillow before she reached to the control to raise the head of the bed. "I wish he hadn't."

"Why?"

"Just because."

"Because why, Leah? We know that you were in foster care. A friend's father who is an investigator has found them and talked to them." At her glare, he held up a hand. "We needed to know, Leah. You couldn't remember anything about your previous life. Not one thing. You didn't even remember your last name."

She sighed, the glare disappearing. "That's okay, Jeremiah, in that case. I remember now." A look of fear fluttered across her face.

"What or who are you afraid of, Leah? Let us help you."

"I can't." Her words were barely above a whisper.

"And why not?" Jeremiah and Leah both jumped at Josh's words.

Jeremiah rose, drawing Josh over to the chair. "I'll be outside. You two can hash this out." He walked away, standing out in the hallway for a moment, before he looked around and headed for the chapel. He needed to spend time in prayer for his friends, but also for his new town and church.

Chapter 9

*W*atching the door close after Jeremiah, Josh stood for a moment, lost in thought, before he turned back to Leah, finding her eyes on him. He sank down into the chair Jeremiah had vacated and studied her.

"How are you feeling?" He had to say something, had to break the silence.

She shrugged. "I have a horrible headache and the vision isn't great. Do you know how sick you can feel from double vision?"

He grinned for a moment. "I do. It's not fun. Other than that, how are you?"

She once more shrugged. "I really don't know." She frowned, even as she studied his face. "I'm sorry, but I take it you're Josh?"

"I am. You don't remember me?" When she shook her head slightly, he smiled. "That's okay. We've only known each other for a couple of days, anyway."

"No, it's not okay. I feel like I should remember you, that you've helped me in some way. Tell me how we met. I can remember your restaurant, I think. Jeremiah said it was yours."

"It was. You ran in the back door, tried to run when I approached you, back out the door again. I caught up with you. I ended up taking you to my house where a friend and his wife met us. We had you checked out by a friend, Doc, who said you had had a concussion. Simon, another friend, found your car, battered and beaten, the windows all broken. We think that's how you ended up with a concussion in the first place. We were walking through the downtown area this morning and when I went to talk to a friend, you disappeared. Somehow you ended up in the old schoolhouse, which collapsed around you."

She stared at him. "There is no way all that happened to me. I don't live that kind of life." She was in shock, her eyes huge.

Josh grinned. "It has. All in the space of say three days, four at the most?"

She shook her head. "There is absolutely no way that would happen. And just why would I go into an old building anyway?"

"Apparently to rescue a kitten you heard, that you decided I needed for my two nieces."

"A kitten? There is no way I'd do that. I don't like cats." She stared as he just shook his head and grinned at her. "No way!" When he still grinned at her, she sighed. "I wouldn't do that. I don't rescue animals. I don't go into old buildings on my own."

"Sorry, Leah. This time you did. And Simon, a friend, had to do some talking to get you to give up the kitten, which by the way is now at my house with my sister and her girls. I don't think I'll get to keep it."

She stared at him, knowing he was telling the truth, but seeing the hint of teasing coming through. She knew from Joy that he could tease but that he loved his sister and nieces dearly. "I still can't see me doing that."

"You did. Unfortunately, it ended up with you here in the hospital. The fire chief is still trying to figure out how the building came down, but they think it was set up to get you into it and then bring the building down on top of you."

She stared at him, horror coursing through her. "Then he really did mean it, didn't he?"

Josh was instantly stern and concerned. "Who, Leah? Who are you talking about?"

She shook her head. "I can't tell you." Her voice was barely above a whisper. "He threatened to kill my foster family. He said he had my real parents somewhere. He won't tell me if they are alive or dead." Tears sparkled in her eyes and Josh reached to grasp her hand, finding hers ice cold.

"Leah, you need to tell someone. We can help you. Please, let us. Let me." Josh knew he was begging but he felt he had no choice.

She shook her head, but it was not as forceful as it had been. "I don't want you hurt, Josh."

"And I don't want to see you hurt, not any worse than you have been." He looked up at the ceiling, as if to ask for help, before looking back at her. "All I ask is that you talk to me. Please. You were coming to Mistletoe for a reason. Maybe if you know why, we can figure out who."

She stared at him for a moment, then sighed. "I was coming to find you, I think. Joy has talked so much about you, I thought maybe you could help me or you would know someone who could. I knew it wasn't a very smart idea, but I didn't know who else to turn to."

"I'm glad you did come, Leah. Let's work through what you know and then go from there."

She nodded, pain flickering across her face. "I will, but right now, I just can't think straight."

Josh stood to leave, to let her sleep, just as she reached for his hand.

"Can you stay for a bit, Josh? I don't want to be alone." He nodded as he sank back into the chair, having to pull it closer to the bed as she pulled on his hand. "Thank you. I'll sleep now." Her eyes slid closed and she slept, her hand with Josh's tight in it curled up under her cheek as she turned to her side.

Josh gave a small smile and tried to pull his hand back, finding she would not release his. This is great, he thought. Now what do I do?

He waited for a while and once more tried to free his hand, without success. He sighed and then carefully moved her fingers to release his hand, sitting back in the chair before he rose and quietly placed the chair back to where it usually sat. He stood, his eyes on her, then moved to the door, stopping once more to look back at her before he looked up and seemed to receive confirmation of something.

Simon stood outside the door, waiting for him, and followed Josh back to his room. Josh dropped down on the edge of the bed, feeling restless and in danger, but not knowing why.

"How is she?" Simon studied his friend with concern, seeing something in his face Josh didn't realize he showed.

"She really doesn't remember the last few days. She also says she wouldn't have gone in to find a kitten." He smiled at Simon's snort of laughter.

"Well, she did. I had to take it from her, remember?"

"I do, from what you said. Now, she says someone threatened her foster family and that they know where her real family is."

Simon sat up straighter in the chair he had dropped into. "Say what?"

Josh repeated himself. "Just what I said. She also said she was coming here to find me, hoping I could help or one of my friends could. That I don't get."

"Joy." Josh stared at Simon. "Joy's talked about you. She's talked about your friends. So it would make sense that Leah would head away from home to find someone to help her."

Josh shrugged. "I guess. Or the girls. Maybe even Jeremiah. I still don't get it though." He paused, his thoughts drifting to something else. "Did you find Donald?"

"No, and that concerns me. We still need to talk to him about what happened with Blackie and Julia last year. We've never been able to."

"No. That was strange, sending them out on that rescue mission, and then disappearing. Did Samuel ever track down his family connection to here?"

"There is none. Donald showed up here about five years ago, became involved in the search and rescue team, and then sort of took it over when the leader retired. He was never formally voted in as leader, and with what he did to Julia, that has rankled a number of the members."

Josh stared at the floor, his arms folded across his chest, as he became lost in thought. Simon watched him, concern in his own eyes for his friend. Just how far is he into this, Lord, Simon asked.

Simon's head turned slightly as he heard soft footsteps walking towards them. Samuel stood for a moment before he reached for a second chair, startling Josh as he did so.

"Samuel! I didn't hear you."

Samuel laughed. "No, I didn't think you did. You were pretty lost in thought. Now, I know you've been to talk to Leah. What can you share?"

Josh sighed, his eyes resting on Simon, who nodded. "I did speak with her. She really doesn't remember the last couple of days. But she is terrified of someone who threatened to kill her foster family, said he knew where her real parents were and that she headed to Mistletoe to find me or one of my friends for help. Does that sound about right?" He looked over at Samuel, catching a slight smile on his face and then frowned. "Samuel?"

"Josh?"

"Oh, and she would never have gone into a building like that, particularly to rescue a cat. She doesn't like them."

Samuel started laughing at that, causing Simon to join him, and then finally Josh.

"Did she really say that?" Samuel's voice held a question he didn't ask.

"She did. I have no idea why she doesn't but that's what she said. Maybe something to ask her family." Josh sighed and then crawled up on the bed, pulling the covers over himself. He was exhausted but not ready to sleep.

"Josh?" Samuel's voice caught his attention and he looked at him, seeing the concern there.

"I'm okay, Samuel. Just tired. Whatever it was they gave me hasn't worn off yet."

Simon began to laugh once more. "Man, you should have seen yourself. You were so determined to get up, we could barely keep you on the ground." He sobered. "That's when you said you knew who was after her. Is that what you meant when you said Donald?"

Josh nodded. "It is. He was there. I can't prove he had anything to do with what happened, though, and I may never."

Samuel shook his head. "Leave it with us and the police, Josh. We have the resources we need. You have enough with your restaurant right now."   A spark of mischief lit up his face, making him look a lot like Blackie.   "Besides, you have an eight-week-old kitten to name and look after."

Josh groaned as he laid his head back. "Please, do not remind me of that. I can't have a cat in the house."

"And why not?"

Josh shook his head at Simon's question. "I just can't. Besides, I think the girls would be disappointed not to take it with them. After all, she rescued it for me to give to them." He smirked as the two with him broke out into laughter again, hushing as the door squeaked open and the nurse entered.

"Do you need anything, Josh?   No? By the way, this was left for you."   She dropped an envelope on the table and then walked out.

Josh stared at the envelope, not making any effort to touch it.   Simon reached into his pocket, felt around and pulled out latex gloves, reaching for the letter at Josh's nod.

Simon studied the envelope, seeing Josh's name written in bold block letters. No much help there, he thought. Unable to trace this more than likely. He flipped the envelope over, finding the flap sealed, and reached into his pocket for his knife.

Slitting open the envelope, he hesitated, his eyes first on Josh, who had sat back up, watching with interesting Simon's movements, and then turning to Samuel, who frowned, seeming to know that whatever the envelope contained, it would change the direction of their investigation and he wasn't ready for that to happen yet.

$\mathcal{J}$osh watched as Simon carefully extracted the paper folded inside, not quite sure what he was facing with it. Simon shot a look at the two men with him before he carefully unfolded it, a frown covering his face.

"Simon?" Josh's voice caught his attention.

"It's blank, Josh. Absolutely nothing on it that I can see. What in the world is going on?"

Samuel stood at Simon's side, his eyes on the paper, watching carefully as Simon flipped it over to inspect the other side. A frown covered his face as a memory niggled at his mind.

"I've seen this before, Josh, Simon. It's been years. Don't tell me he's back."

"Who's back, Samuel?"

"We had an investigation about fifteen years ago. A client would receive letters like this, meant to terrorize them, and it did. There was never anything on the paper. We did every test imaginable to try and bring up words, DNA, anything. Nothing could be found. I suspect that's what your lab will find with that." He pointed to the paper. "And the envelope will be the same. You'll get nothing from the printing."

"So, what happened?" Josh was deeply concerned, knowing that terror would not sit well with him when it came to Leah.

"The letters stopped. It took a good while for my client to get their life back. We had looked into everyone they had contact with and found no one that would have sent something like this."

"But with Leah, you're thinking differently." Simon's keen eyes studied the older man, catching the look in his eyes that said he was.

"I am, Simon. Given what's gone on with her, I would say it is different. I had a chance to speak with your police chief tonight before I came back. It was deliberate, the way the building came down.

Someone placed tiny ribbons of explosives in the corners and then laid almost invisible wires from them to the centre of the floor. He thinks that when Leah walked across it, she would step on a sensor and set off a small charge, likely no louder than a pop. He's planning on talking to her to see if she can remember anything."

"That makes sense." Simon studied Josh, who nodded. "It would have to be someone who knows explosives to do something that sophisticated, don't you think?"

Samuel shook his head. "Not necessarily. The internet is a good source of information nowadays, unfortunately. They look for the right wording and they'll find what they want."

Josh nodded, folding his arms back across his chest, and laying his head on the pillow. "I suspect she really won't remember much. Not right now, anyway. She doesn't remember going into the building or rescuing the kitten. She doesn't remember meeting me at all." They could hear the pain in Josh's voice at that sentence and knew that he had found his treasure, his lady, but would he be hers, that was the question unanswered.

Samuel finally stood, staring down at the blank sheet of paper, a frown on his face. "There's something about that paper, Simon, something I'm just not remembering right at the moment. It will come to me." He looked up at Josh. "How serious was she when she said she thought her parents were still alive?"

He shrugged. "I can't tell. I don't know her that well. Ask Joy or Jeremiah. They might have a better read than I do." He sighed. "Just get me out of here, please?"

"Tomorrow, my friend. Then, we'll have to find a place for Leah to stay." Simon held up his hand. "I know Joy and Jeremiah are planning on staying with you for a while. That would work for the first few days. But we really need to find somewhere she'll be safe."

"Yeah, and where's that, Simon? Look what happened with both Jacob and Blackie. They certainly weren't safe. Or Blackie's friends, Cara and Corin."

"No, they weren't." Samuel stood for a moment, eyes on him. "But we'll do our best for your lady, Josh. You can depend on that."

Josh finally nodded. "I know, Samuel. I know you'll do your best. But look at what just happened to her. How do we keep her safe?"

Samuel and Simon exchanged glances, both wondering just how deep Josh's feelings went and just what he would do to keep his lady safe.

They turned as they heard the door open. Then Josh was off the bed and at Leah's side, a smile on his face, but also a questioning look.

"Leah?"

She looked up at him, fear evident on her face. "He was in my room, Josh. I pretended to be asleep, but he was there. I heard him talking to me, telling me I was no good, that I had to be taken care of, just like my parents." Tears sparkled in her eyes, tears that soon overflowed, no matter how much she determined that they not.

Josh gave an inaudible sound and swept her into a hug, turning slightly so he could see the other two men. Simon nodded, already heading out the door to find the officer who should have been at her door.

"Was the officer there when you came out?"

"Officer? What officer? There wasn't anyone in the hall. I just knew you were here somewhere and looked for you." She stared up at him, a frown now on her face. "Why would there be an officer at my door?"

"To protect you, Leah." Samuel gave a gentle smile as she started and then turned to face him, Josh's arms loosening enough so she could.

"I'm sorry?"

"I'm Blackie's father, Samuel. I didn't mean to frighten you. Here. Sit in this chair." Samuel grabbed a blanket and wrapped her in it before she sat, taking care of her just as he would one of his own two daughters.

Josh's hands stayed on her shoulders as he stood behind her, his eyes on her head. Why, Lord, was his question. Can she not have peace of some kind? What is this all about anyway? He felt a peace flow through him, felt the confidence that God really was in control, that no matter what happened, God would walk every step with them.

He felt Leah moving restlessly under his hands and stepped back, his eyes on Samuel, who was studying Leah.

"Leah. What can you tell us about this man?" Samuel glanced up as he heard Simon and then the police chief entering the room. He sighed. This is not the quiet hospital room she should be in. We need to get her out of here, he thought.

She shook her head. "I didn't see him. I just heard him and felt his hand on my arm. He squeezed it as he spoke." She paused, a frown on her face as she thought back over the event. "I am almost sure I know the voice, but I just can't place it. I know I've heard it somewhere."

Samuel shared a glance with Josh and then Simon and Ed. "I suggest we remove Leah from the hospital and take her somewhere we have better control over her visitors. Josh?"

"I agree. My place is fairly secure. It had a good security system already installed when I moved in."

Ed nodded. "The man who had it before you worked for the government and needed extra security. But I am not convinced that will be enough."

Josh was watching him and sighed when he realized what he meant. Was he ready for that step, with someone who didn't know him, didn't remember that he had helped her?

"What happened to the officer, Ed?" Josh instead asked another question.

"He was knocked out. No one saw anything. He's still out, so I can't question him." Ed turned slightly as he heard a tap at the door and cracked it open. "I'll be back. See if you can come up with a plan in the mean while."

Simon turned back from the door, his eyes on Samuel, who nodded towards Josh.

"Josh, can I talk to you for a moment? Let's get Leah back to her room and let her get dressed. We're moving her tonight."

Leah stared up at Simon. "Moving me? The doctor won't let me go. He said so."

"He will. I'll personally talk to him. It's more important that we keep you alive than you stay here. And somehow I don't think you will be alive come morning unless we do move you." Simon hated to scare her but knew he had no choice, seeing her face whiten as his words.

Leah finally stood, Josh's hand on her back as he guided her back to her room, Simon having already searched it.

"I'll be right outside, Leah. Just open the door when you're ready. Do you need me to get the nurse for you?"

She shook her head, regretting doing just that. "No, I think I'll be okay. I'll need help with my shoes, though."

"Come get me." Josh pulled the door closed behind her.

Simon watched as Josh hesitated outside the door, before walking down the hall towards him. Samuel stood guard for Leah, as did the police chief. Josh stopped just inside his room door, searching for what he didn't know, before he reached for his clothes and dressed, leaving the hospital pyjamas and robe on the bed.

"Let's get us out of here, Simon."

Simon's hand came out to stop Josh. "Josh, we need a plan. We can't just wing it, you know."

Josh shook his head. "I have no plan, other than to get Leah to my place. From there, we'll discuss what we need to do."

Simon watched his friend intently. "I know you, Josh. You already have a plan."

Josh shook his head. "No, I don't. Not really. Other than to marry her and take her away from here."

"That won't work, you know."

"What, marrying her?" Josh stared at his friend, seeing the concern there.

"That. And taking her away. He'd just follow you. We need to find out who is it and stop him. Now."

"Before Christmas, please."   Josh shrugged into his jacket, his hands shoving into his pocket to reach for his gloves. "What's this?"   He pulled out an envelope. "Not another one."

Simon reached for it, knowing there would be no use trying to protect it now. "Let me see it, please."   Opening it, he found once more a blank piece of paper. "This is so bizarre.   He's got you on his radar now.   That makes two of you to keep safe."

"And you're going to say you can't do that with us in two different places."   He waved his hand as he walked away, intent on finding Leah.

Leah watched as Josh knelt to tie her shoes, not liking that he had to do that for her, but on the other hand, liking the courtesy he was showing her.   Something softened inside her at his actions.

He stood, his eyes on her, seeing the pain in them but also the fear.   There was something else he couldn't read, not yet anyway.

"Ready to go?"

She nodded and took the hand he held out for her. "Where to, Josh?"

"Back to my place for now. We need to talk, you and I."

She sighed. "I know we do. Can we in the morning?" She leaned against him for a moment, not even aware that she had. "I'm just so tired, Josh. Tired of running and hiding. I haven't seen my family in years now, not wanting to be near them. I haven't even dared to call."

"We'll get you together. Trust me on that." He released her hand and drew an arm around her. "Lean on me. We're going down the service elevator, Simon tells me."

Chapter 11

Dumfounded, Leah stood in Josh's home office and stared at him late the next afternoon. She had slept late that morning, needing the rest, and had just finally began to feel somewhat like herself again. Joy had told her that Josh had headed into his restaurant early that morning, wanting to talk with her but needing to be there. She shook her head at what he had asked.

"Josh! That's not what we need to do!" She was in shock, she thought. Lord, how did I get here?

Josh ran his hand through his hair as he watched her begin to pace. This was not how he had planned to talk to her. Joy had left with the two girls, with the understanding they'd be back in an hour or so. She had pointed at Leah, letting him know he needed to address the issue with her, whatever the issue was.

"Leah. I know it's not what you expected. Just listen to me for a moment." He paused, gathering his thoughts. He really needed to talk to his father right about now and that man was still on the road to Mistletoe.

"You're absolutely right, Josh. How can you even begin to ask that question?" She turned, a puzzled look on her face, as she stopped in front of him. "We don't know each other well enough to even consider marrying one another."

Josh nodded. "I know we don't. I'm just trying to come up with a way to keep you safe. I thought that would be one way. I guess not." He turned away, swallowing hard against his disappointment and worry, and moved towards the door. He paused for a moment, then, shaking his head, continued to walk away.

Leah watched him go, her hand on her mouth. She had just received a marriage proposal, she thought, not at all like she had ever dreamed of, though. Lord, what do I do? You know his heart. I don't. I know I have no one else who would even offer his hand to me in such a way. She sighed, her eyes searching the room, seeing Josh's Bible on his desk. She walked over to the desk, her hand resting on the Book and then picking it up, settled herself in an easy chair near the fireplace he had lit earlier. She leafed through the book, finally settling on a favourite chapter, the words filling her with hope and courage. She closed her eyes, her head bowed over the Book, not seeing Josh pause at the doorway on his way back in to apologize to her and say he would come up with another way to ensure her safety. He turned, seeking his own prayer corner. This was not an easy decision for either one of them.

Joy stopped as she saw her brother in the kitchen, standing, coffee pot in hand, staring out the back window, and just shook her head. She knew their parents were due in at any time and she had to prepare him for that. It's what she did as the older sibling. It had been hard when he had been in the armed forces, away for eight years, home for just brief visits. Then when he moved to Mistletoe once he was out, she had felt like he had abandoned her. She knew he hadn't, that he had had a reason for coming here.

She just didn't see it or maybe it was that she didn't want to see it.

"Josh?" Her soft question startled him and water sloshed from the coffee pot onto the counter. He filled the reservoir on the maker and set the coffee to perk, reaching for a cloth to wipe up the water.

"Joy? Where are the girls?"

"With Jeremiah. They decided they wanted to do some shopping and he volunteered to help them. I have no idea what they'll come home with." She laughed at the thought, causing him to grin slightly. "What about you? Are you okay?"

He sighed, giving a small shrug. "I don't know, Joy." He looked at her, a bleakness around his eyes she had never seen before. "I just don't know how to keep Leah safe. We have no idea who it is or why, other than it might be related to her last name and this town." He turned, anger emanating from him for a moment. "There are times I wish I had never heard of this town."

Joy's arm went around her brother as she hugged him, her head resting on his arm. "We'll get there, brother. Just let God lead."

"I know that, Joy. I just don't see it right now." He paused as he heard a small sound behind him and glanced over his shoulder, seeing Leah standing in the doorway, hesitation in her manner. He turned, dislodging Joy's arm, and leaned back against the counter. "Leah?"

"Josh? Can we talk?" She was distraught, he could tell as he walked towards her, following her back to the office.

He shut the door behind him, knowing this was one conversation they needed to have in private.

"Leah? What's up?"

Leah walked to stand in front on him, her arms folded around herself, her eyes raised to his. "I've thought about what you asked. I've also spent time in prayer. I know what that answer is, but I'm still so unsure of anything." Tears sparkled in her eyes but she stepped back as he reached for her. "Please. Just let me say my piece."

Josh nodded. "Sure." He tilted his head to watch her face. "That is, if you're going to talk."

She shook her head at his gentle teasing, knowing it came from his tender heart and a desire to ease the situation for her.

"I know why you asked what you did. I'm just not convinced that's the way we should go. I'm not even sure I should be making a decision about a lifelong commitment when I have a head injury." She turned and paced away, stopping with her back to him. "If your question is still on the table, then my answer would be yes."

Josh stood motionless, stunned at her response. It was not what he had expected her to say. "Leah? You're saying yes? You're sure?"

He watched as she hesitated, then nodded her head, her dark red curls shaking with the movement of her head. "I am, Josh. God alone knows why I am, but after praying and waiting, I have a peace that's what we should do." She turned. "I'm just not sure at all, though."

He smiled as he walked towards her, his hands coming down on her shoulders. "One step, one day at a time, sweetheart. That's all we can do." He turned his head slightly as he heard commotion in the hallway. "I think Mom and Dad have just arrived." His hands tightened on her shoulders as she gasped and tried to move back. "You know them, Leah. They will welcome you to their hearts, if they haven't already." His hand slid down her arm and to her hand. "Come. I have something for you."

She sat in his desk chair as he gently pushed her down, her eyes following him as he opened a drawer and pulled out a jeweller's box.

"My grandmother gave me this. Told me it was a treasure for my treasured one." He lifted solemn eyes to Leah as he opened it, to show a beautiful emerald stone in a unique setting. "Gramps bought it for her when they were first married, once he could afford to get her an engagement ring." He paused, his eyes dropping back to the ring. "I know what we're doing is unorthodox. That we don't know each other that well." He raised eyes to hers again. "Will you wear it for me? Wear it as a sign of your trust and faith in me? For now?"

She finally nodded and he reached for her hand.   "I promise, Leah, to do everything in my power to protect you, to keep you safe, to learn to love you as I should." He stooped, dropping a kiss on her forehead.

"Thank you, Josh." Her words were barely audible. "I just don't know, though."

"I know, sweetheart. I know. Let's just see how it goes." He turned his head to look at the door. "They'll want to know why and when."

She shook in her anxiety and he drew her up into his arms. She relaxed against him, feeling his strength and courage and determination to keep her safe. "I guess then we need to set a date." She leaned back. "How do we even do that?"

"Let's wait for a day or two and see what happens. If Simon and the chief are able to find the man or men responsible, then there will be no rush. But if things escalate, we'll need to talk again."

She nodded, burrowing against him, hiding her face and the fear she felt. "Okay, then. Let's go face your family." She leaned back again as she felt his body shaking with laughter. "What did I say that's so funny?"

"It sounded like you were walking out to face a judge and jury. You're not. They all love you now. The girls will be over the moon ecstatic."

"That's what I'm afraid of, Josh. I'm afraid I'll disappoint them." She moved to walk towards the door, stopping as his arms surrounded her again.

"Never think like that. You will never disappoint us with this. Even if we both walk away from each other once you're safe, it will not be a disappointment. They understand." He waited until she nodded. "I talked to Simon today. He'll be by later with the chief. They both want to talk to you. But if you're too tired, let me know. You still need a lot of rest, given your head injury. If anything, I'll take you with me to the restaurant tomorrow and they can come talk to you there."

"That might be best, Josh. I'm feeling a trifle overwhelmed right at the moment."

He nodded, his chin brushing against her hair, even as he bowed his head and prayed.

He reached for her hand as they walked towards the kitchen and the laughter and talking they could hear, intermingled with the excited squeals of the girls. He glanced down at her just before he reached the doorway and squeezed her hand.

"Just remember. We're in this together, sweetheart. Together with God."

She nodded, fright flickering across her face for a moment before she seemed to steel herself.

Josh's mother looked up as she heard their footsteps and was across the room to hug her son. Martha held tight for a moment, before she stepped back, her eyes on his face and then nodding. She turned to the woman beside him, surprise on her face.

"Leah? Oh, how nice. Joy mentioned you were in town. I just wasn't expecting to see you here." She looked between Josh and

Leah even as Josh's dad, Andrew, greeting his son. "Josh? What's going on?"

Josh stepped back to Leah's side, his arm going around her. "We'll explain later, but Leah has done me the honour of agreeing to marry me."

Gasps could be heard from his parents even as talk broke out. His eyes sought Jeremiah and saw his nod, knowing they would talk later.

Later, as Joy and her mother were with the girls, Andrew and Jeremiah turned to the younger couple.

"Josh, I think you need to explain."

Before Josh could explain, the doorbell rang. He rose, returning with Simon and the police chief. Andrew stayed for a while, then excused himself, heading to the garage apartment. Somehow, he knew his son was in trouble and he needed to spend time in prayer.

Josh finally locked the door. Simon and Ed had little new to add to what they had already talked about. He leant his head against the door for a moment, suddenly exhausted beyond belief. He needed to sleep but didn't know if he could. Leah, he knew, had retired as had the rest of the household.

He yawned, stopping mid-yawn as he heard a voice behind him. He spun, seeing Jeremiah standing here.

"I thought you had gone to bed."

"I hadn't. I just wanted to catch you before tomorrow. I know you're planning on taking Leah with you to the restaurant. I'll stop by mid-morning, if you think it will be quiet enough for us to talk. We do need to talk." Jeremiah's heart was troubled for the man he called brother.

"That should be fine. Night." Josh walked by him, feeling Jeremiah's hand on his shoulder for a brief moment. He shuddered with fear suddenly as he closed the door to his bedroom, not knowing exactly why, but knowing that by taking the step they had, they had just opened themselves up to more trouble.

Chapter 12

Laughing at Amy's teasing, Josh shook his head the next morning, even as his mind sorted through the lack of information regarding Leah's assailant. He wanted this over for her. She needed that. He sighed to himself. *Lord, I know it's Your timing. Can we just get through this quickly?*

He finally stood in his office doorway, a puzzled look on his face. Leah was seated at his desk and he could see stacks of papers around her. He moved forward, seeing that she had organized his mail and whatever other paperwork he had dropped there three days ago.

She looked up, a smile on her face, then a look of uncertainty. "I thought I was helping you, Josh. Just organizing things for you." She went to rise from his chair but his hand on her arm stopped her.

"That's fine, Leah. I like that you just went ahead." He turned to look at his desk, perching on a corner. "Oh, wonderful. I see you've found the chequebook too and have the cheques ready. That is a huge help. Now I'm not going to be stuck here until early evening catching up." His grin warmed her heart.

"You really don't mind?"

He shook his head. "Not at all. It's nice to have this all taken care of. I'll unlock the filing cabinet for you as well." He reached into the desk drawer and pulled out a set of keys. "Here. These are the building keys. This little one is the filing cabinet. Take them and keep them with you at all times."

"Are you sure?" She really hadn't expected that response from him.

"I am." He grinned at her. "Here, let me grab a pen and I'll sign off on the cheques. Boot up the computer and I'll walk you through my accounting program." He showed her the program, pleased to hear that she knew it from her previous employment. "What about your job, Leah?"

"Oh, that. I quit it just before I left town. I wanted a change." She looked around the office. "How do you manage to do all that you do?"

"It's been hard. The House was losing money when I took it over but I've turned that around. I have great staff, who really care about the people they serve." He looked down at the cheques, then back at her. "I'll employ you here, Leah. I could use someone to do my paperwork and ordering. I think you'd be perfect at it."

She sat back, her eyes on him. "I accept, if you're sure." Her eyes narrowed. "Unless it's just a ploy to keep track of me."

He started to laugh, shaking his head. "That too, but I really would like it if you were working here. It would make my day go faster."

She nodded. "Okay, then. I guess you have a secretary. I'd feel safer tucked away in here too. They'd have to go through a few people to get to me."

He laughed even as he reached for the employee file. "Now, all I have to do are the employees' cheques. They're due out today. Work with me on them, and then next week you're on your own with them."

Josh finally headed back to the kitchen, his mind already on that, leaving Leah to stare after him, then down at the desk he had left cluttered behind him. She sighed and began the task of folding invoice copies around cheques and addressing envelopes.

She finally wandered towards the kitchen, standing back where she couldn't be seen, watching as Josh flipped burgers, plated specials and generally kept flying around the room, stopping every once in a while to wipe his hands on his apron, all the time a smile on his face and teasing words for his staff. She could tell he was respected, that the staff were working their hardest for him.

How will what we're going through change this, Lord? I don't want him hurt, but that's exactly what I fear will happen.

She stepped forward towards the doorway and then froze, a voice reaching to her ears. He was here, she thought. I'm not even safe here. She turned and almost ran for the office, shutting the door behind her and sliding down the wall to sit with her head on her upraised knees, arms tight around her legs. Amy caught sight of her turning and fleeing and turned to find Josh, taking the spatula from his hand with a quiet word and nod towards his office.

Josh hit the office doorway almost on a run, carefully opening the door and searching for Leah. Finding her, he sank down to sit crosslegged on the floor, pulling her onto his lap, his arms wrapped around her, just holding her as she shuddered in shock.

Amy appeared at the door, heading for the closet and the blanket Josh asked her to bring him. She stood, watching as Josh talked with Leah, finally getting a response.

"What happened, Leah? What scared you?"

She looked up at him, Amy seeing the stark fear on her face. "He's in the restaurant, Josh. I heard his voice."

Josh froze for a moment, his eyes on his beloved's face before they raised to Amy.

"Amy, we need the names of everyone who is in the restaurant right now, local or stranger. Come up with something that gets you that information, a free meal, meal on

131

the house next visit, whatever. And call Chief Waters. I need to talk to him."

"On it, boss." Amy was away, not asking why Josh needed the information, just willing to do what she could for him.

The chief paced Josh's office, his eyes on the paper Amy had handed him as he approached her. He shook his head. Who would have thought the man would have been so bold? He doubted that the name was there, but he still had to go over the list with Leah, and that didn't look like it was happening in the near future.

Josh covered Leah's sleeping form with the blanket as she lay on the couch in his office before he turned.

"Now what, Ed? He was here. He knows where to find her. How?"

Ed shrugged. "He knows she's with you. It's not hard to figure out where you'd be." He held up the list. "I need to talk to her about this."

"I know you do." Josh sighed. "This is not how I envisioned today."

"What do you mean?" Ed looked between Josh and Leah, not quite understanding.

"I just hired her to work here." Josh didn't say what he really wanted to say, that he had found the love of his life, his treasure, and she had agreed to be his. That wouldn't go over well, he knew.

"That's a good thought, Josh. You can tuck her away here. But obviously someone else has thought of her being here." Ed paced, finally stopping at Josh's desk.

"Where's the list, Josh?"

Josh spun at Leah's words, not realizing she had awakened and sat up while the men were conversing.

"Leah. You're awake. Here, it is." Josh sat beside her as he handed it to her. "Do you recognize any names?"

She started to shake her head, then paused. "This one. Donald. I'm sure it's his voice that I've heard, that he's the one who has been terrorizing me. Who is he?"

"Someone we would really like to talk with. We're finding out he's not who he has said he is." The chief looked grim. "It was really bold of him to come back into town like that, given how the feeling is about him here."

Josh stared at Leah for a moment before he stood, motioning with his head for Ed to follow him out of the room. He stood where he could watch Leah, nodding as Amy approaching and then went to sit with Leah

"Is he really that bold?" Josh was unsettled.

"It looks as if he is. I have patrols out looking for him now, just from what you said happened when Leah was hurt. No, we haven't found him. He was in town long enough to find some holes to disappear down in." Ed paused. "I wonder if Old Jack has seen him."

"I haven't seen Jack in a couple of days. But then again that's not unusual." Josh didn't continue, not knowing how much Ed knew or had guessed about Old Jack's connection to town.

Chapter 13

That night, his three friends, Jeremiah, and his father stood in his kitchen, staring at him, not quite sure to believe what Josh had just said. Joy and his mother had Leah up in the garage apartment, with the little girls, wrapping presents for the youth centre Blackie ran.

"He was in the restaurant?" Simon stared at Josh, who was also watched by Jacob.

"He was that bold. The staff wouldn't have known we wanted to talk to him. I spoke with each one and advised them that if he comes in again, they serve him but call in the police, detaining him until they arrive." Josh turned to pace, worry on his face. "Now, how do I keep Leah safe? We're not sure he knew she was there. She was tucked back in the office all day."

Blackie shook his head. "He's bold, I must say that for him. Did Amy say if she recognized him at all?"

"I didn't get a chance to ask her, but she wasn't out on the floor much, more in the kitchen." Josh sighed as he ran a hand through his hair, lost for a moment as to what to do. "Dad? What do you suggest?"

His father nodded, then pointed to a chair. "Why don't we sit? I, for one, want to get off my feet. Your mother's had me running around all day, Josh, and my feet are very tired." He took the coffee mug he was offered by Jacob with a quiet thanks. He raised his eyes to his son, seeing Josh staring down at his own mug, lost to them for a moment, his hand reaching for the little kitten as she crawled up his leg and settled down on his arm. Lord, what I am about to say is going to shock him, I know, and it will change his life. I just don't know how to word it. This time, it has to be Your words, not mine.

"Josh?" Andrew waited until Josh looked up at him. "How serious are you about Leah? I know this is a conversation you and I need to have in private as well, but just let me know it's serious and we'll go on from there."

Josh kept his eyes on his father, not saying a word, his father reading his answer in his eyes before he nodded.

"All right, then. We'll talk later, son. There are some things we do need to decide now though." Andrew had been in law enforcement in his earlier years before he retired to run a book store he had inherited from his mother. "Where do you see this going, Simon?"

Simon sighed. "I have no idea at present, Andrew. We do know that Leah is connected to the town, as one of the descendants from the Bronagh family. We're still working through that relationship, but she is a cousin of sorts to both Julia and Finn, even though it is more distant than that of Julia and Finn to one another. We have been searching for Donald without any luck in finding him."

Josh turned to his friend. "Have you searched the outlying sheds and cabins? I know Donald had a connection to one way back in the bush."

"We've been there and seen evidence someone has been living there, but he wasn't around. We'll be watching it though." Simon turned to Blackie. "What about any of your kids at the centre? Have they said anything?"

Blackie shook his head. "No, and they would come to me if they had. Julia's really popular with the girls and they trust her. They would let her know that Donald was around. They all know what happened to her."

Josh finally rose, not happy that there was nothing they could plan for, nothing concrete they could decide. Simon was right, once again, he thought. There really isn't that much evidence, and I know he's been speaking with Ed. Dad's right, too. Now what, Lord? Where do I go from here?

He rinsed the mugs they had used and stacked them into the dishwasher, reaching under the sink for more detergent to set the machine running. He heard his father's quiet footsteps behind him and then a chair as it gently scraped back across the tiled floor.

He turned, seeing his father's eyes not on him as he expected, but on his Bible. Josh sighed, knowing that the inevitable talk was on the table, and he would have to own up to his feelings about Leah. He slid into a seat across from his father, knowing they likely didn't have a long time to talk. Joy would be back with the girls soon for bed.

Andrew finally looked up at his son, a sigh rising within him. Where do I go with this, Lord? I don't know how to read him now, not in this situation. I know he has a good heart, that he's a man of God.

"Dad? You wanted to talk?" Josh watched as his father finally nodded, his hands folded on his open Bible.

"I do, son, and now I'm not sure how to proceed."

"At the beginning would be a good place as you are wont to say." Josh grinned at his father, receiving an answering grin and a shake of the head in response.

"That's too true. I know how you and Leah met. I know somewhat of the trouble you two are facing. It concerns me that you really don't know her that well, not well enough to take such a big step."

Josh sighed, then nodded. "I know, Dad. It's tough to explain. I am not even sure if I can. It's just that….It seems….." Josh's voice finally died way.

Andrew's soft smile caught Josh's attention and he frowned at his father.

"Dad?"

"You've got it bad, son, don't you? She has you at a loss for words. I was like that when I met your mother. I stumbled over my words all the time. Just couldn't put a sentence together that made sense. Even today, I sometimes look at her and feel the same."

Josh sat back, relief coursing through him that his father understood. "Thanks, Dad. That does help." He nodded towards the Bible. "You've found a verse for me, haven't you?"

Andrew nodded, even as the back door opened and the two little girls flew in, excitement wafting from them as they swarmed their grandfather and uncle, sure of their reception, their chatter about the presents they had just helped to wrap.

"We'll talk later, son."

Josh nodded as he slid his chair back so Heidi could sit on his knee, the kitten now nestled in her arms before it scrambled onto Josh's shoulder, where she thought she'd be safe, drawing a pout from Heidi.

Leah stood for a moment, just inside the door, her hands stilled as she reached to hang up her jacket. Josh was laughing at Heidi as he tried to rescue the kitten from his shoulder. She smiled, realizing that she really did have a knight in shining armour after all, didn't she? She caught a glimpse of a future child, their child, with Josh acting the same way. She just didn't know how bad it would get, not knowing who was after her and not knowing when they would strike again.

She turned as Joy spoke to her, nodding at her word of thanks. She passed the men, heading for her bedroom, not realizing that Josh followed her with his eyes before he turned to answer his mother's question. The four other adults in the room shared a look and a smile, not wanting to speak until the girls had been put to bed.

Josh finally tracked Leah down in his home office. She had seated herself at his desk, a book open in front of her. He dropped into a chair across from her, not speaking, just watching her.

"Josh? What do you know of the history of Mistletoe? I'm told I'm related to the founder but I don't see that at all."

He nodded at the book she had open in front of her. "That tells a lot. Finn's parents know a whole lot more. Why don't we drop in on them tomorrow and talk with them?"

"We can't just drop in on someone like that!" She was horrified at the thought.

Josh reached to grasp her hand, his warm and comforting on hers. "This is a different town than you've lived in, Leah. We can do just that. We can drop in on them without any problems. If you like, I'll call Mary in the morning and make sure she'll be home, but I'm sure she will be. At this time of year, their B&B is booked solid and she's around for their clients."

Leah stared at him, then finally nodded, a shuttered look coming over her face.

"Leah, please don't shut me out. Talk to me." Josh's hand tightened on hers.

She finally sighed, her eyes on his hand. "I really don't know what to think anymore, Josh. You've offered me safety through marriage. You provided work for me. Your family have practically adopted me." She held up a hand as he went to speak, causing a grin to spread across his face. She fought an answering smile. Somehow, he really did make her feel safe and secure, and yes loved and wanted just for being her. "I really don't get it. Why?"

"Why? Which question do you want me to answer?"

"I didn't know I had asked more than one, but I guess I sort of did." She looked down as she felt something brush against her foot. "There's your kitten, Josh. Somehow, I don't think she'll be heading out with the girls when Jeremiah and Joy move into their new home on the weekend."

He reached for the little kitten. "Somehow, I think you're right. You really wanted her for them, you know?" He grinned as she shook her head at him. "We need to name her."

"Terror would likely fit in a few weeks. She's got that look in her eyes, but we can't be outside calling for Terror, now can we?" Her eyes on the kitten, she didn't see the swift startled look Josh sent her, not realizing what she had just said. "I'll come up with a name, seeing as I found her." She smirked at his grin. "That's my privilege, you know." She reached for the kitten who mewed in protest about leaving Josh. "She really is your kitten, isn't she? Now, back to the town. You tell me I'm related to one of the founders, through my last name. Is that why I'm under attack?"

Josh nodded. "It could well be. Julia and Finn went through the same thing." He looked up at her gasp. "I'm sorry. We never told you, did we? Last year about this time, someone tried to kill both Finn and Jacob, then a week or two later, Blackie and Julia. It all goes back to the founding fathers and the town charter. People think they can circumvent a legal document, which has been tried and proven in court to be legal. Because you are a direct descendant (Samuel's proven this), you are entitled to some of the town buildings and there is a bank account with your name on it. I have no idea how much is there, or how many buildings." He sat back, his eyes now on the floor. "We'll need to meet with the town lawyer sometime over the next couple of days. Jeremiah and Simon said they'd clear out your apartment for you."

Chapter 14

*L*eaving the town lawyer's office the next afternoon, Leah waited for Josh to open her car door and then close it after she had seated herself. She watched as he rounded the front of the vehicle and then slid inside, his hand inserting the key into the ignition, starting the vehicle, and then just sitting.

"Josh?"

Her question caught his attention, and he turned to her with a smile. "Yes, ma'am?"

She shook her head at him. "You're heading for the restaurant, aren't you?"

He turned to look behind him before he pulled away from his parking spot. "Not now. Amy's on the late shift today and will close up. I usually open and she or Stephen close for me. It's working out well." He stared at her for a second before he looked back out the front window. "Would you care to go out for dinner with me tonight, Leah? Somewhere away from here?"

She stared at him, then nodded. "That would be nice, Josh. Somewhere quiet and sane, perhaps? Is there such a place?"

He began to laugh even as he accelerated away from the edge of town and out to the highway. "Let's go to the next town over. It's not that far, really, not out here. I know a nice quiet restaurant where we can catch an early supper."

Josh prayed as they finished their meal, not he thought as he had ever prayed before, even for his friends on the battlefield. He reached for Leah's hand after their plates had been removed and their coffees refilled.

She watched their linked hands, praying that he wasn't going to say he had made a mistake, that he wanted his freedom back. She had had a peace and feeling of safety in the last few hours that she had not felt in years.

"Leah, I know this is really sudden, what we decided. Dad spoke to me this morning when he stopped by. He asked if we had reconsidered our plans at all. When I said no, he then suggested that we set a date and do so quickly. He feels you may have more safety that way."

She tried to retract her hand but Josh's grip tightened. She stared down at him, worry running over her face, before she looked up, finding his eyes on her, concern in them.

"It has to be your decision, Leah. I am fine with whatever you decide. If you need time to pray about it, then we take that time." He had been praying the whole time he was waiting, asking God to bring them to the right decision.

She finally sighed, her hand relaxing under his before she moved it enough to turn it over and grasp his. "I know where your father's heart is. What does your mother say?" She paused, biting at her lip. "This is so hard, Josh. I need my own parents to talk to, and I don't have them."

"I know, sweetheart. I know. Talk to Mom or to Finn's Mom, if you need to. They'll answer your questions and concerns."

She finally shook her head. "No, I don't think I need to. I think…." Her voice died away as she raised her eyes to stare out the window, straight at a bridal dress shop. She started to giggle, causing Josh to frown and turn to look out as well.

"What's so funny?"

She had trouble containing her mirth. "Look at the shop right across the street, Josh."

When he focused on it, he too began to laugh. "Is that a sign or what?"

She nodded. "I'm guessing it is. So when?"

"This Saturday? Too soon?"

She shook her head, sadness crossing her face. "I wish I had more time, but I don't think we do. I need to find something to wear."

Josh hooked a thumb over his shoulder. "Right there, sweetheart. They're open late by what the sign says. We'll head over there. You pick out your dress, and I won't look." He grinned at her, not seeing the man sitting at a nearby table, his eyes focused on Leah, anger on his face as he watched her.   If she had looked up, she would have recognized him from her past place of employment, and as someone she had feared on the job.

Josh had waited patiently as Leah tried on dresses, finally rising to take the bag from her as she approached him, his arms going out to hug her as he saw the sadness I her eyes.

"I know, sweetheart.   I know.   You need your parents here and they're not.   You need someone to walk you down the aisle, now don't you?"

She nodded her head, then rested her cheek against his chest, not seeing the looks of sympathy the shop owner was sending her.

"Let's go home, Josh.   We can talk about this later."

Josh turned towards Mistletoe, an uneasy feeling in his bones as he watched the traffic around him. It was late afternoon, just beginning to get dusk, and he could feel evil approaching him.   He watched as a vehicle came towards him at high speed before he turned the wheel and headed into a shop parking lot, bringing an exclamation of surprise from Leah.

"Josh?" She stared at him, then out the window.

"Sorry, Leah. Someone was coming at us at a really high speed. I don't think he'd have stopped before he hit us, not with the oncoming traffic." He reached for his phone, making a quick call. "I've asked for a police escort to Mistletoe. They're on their way. Simon has talked to them already, so they've been aware of what we may need."

"And just how did he know that?" She was astounded at the friendship between the four men, never having had that, not really, she thought.

"We're friends, Leah. It's how we are. We help one another." He shot her a quick look even as he caught sight of the marked police cruiser pulling in. "I did let Simon know we were heading this way and I had a bad feeling about something happening."

"Looks as if you were right, doesn't it?" She sat back, a blank look on her face, not letting Josh see how scared she really was.

Josh followed her into his house a while later, his eyes on her, distressed that their happy occasion of dinner had been changed so rapidly. He didn't like it, not one bit. He set the bag with her dress down on her bed, watching as she paced before he reached to hug her. It took a bit but she finally hugged him back. He could feel the faint shivers running through her and decided then and there that he would end this, somehow. He would find the man or woman responsible for this.

Jeremiah turned from the counter to study his brother-in-law as he reached for the coffee pot and filled a mug, setting it down with a loud thump.

"Josh?"

"They followed us, Jeremiah. If I hadn't had a chance to pull into a parking lot, who knows what would have happened?" A dark look covered Josh's face at that.

"Josh, don't do anything foolish or rash. Leave it with the police."

"Well, right now, I don't see them doing that great a job, now, are they?" He sighed, shame running through him. "I'm sorry, Jeremiah. That's not true. I know they're doing the best they can. This just scared me."

Jeremiah nodded. "I know it did, and it will continue until the culprit is under arrest." He looked at the kitchen doorway where Joy stood, the two girls on either side of her. He lowered his voice. "My girls are here. I don't want the little ones scared any more than they have been."

"I won't. I promise. It's likely good that you're moving out on the weekend. Things seem to be heating up."

"But where does that leave you?" Jeremiah shared another look with Joy, puzzled as to what Josh and Leah had planned.

"Joy, go find Leah. See what she found today and let her know how beautiful she is. I can't tell her, not yet. I haven't seen it." Josh sent his sister a smile, one that didn't reach his eyes. He watched as Joy and the girls left to find Joy.

"What did you two go and do?" Jeremiah hooked a chair leg with his foot, pulling out the chair and then dropping down. It had been a long day for him, trying to get an understanding of the church.

"Leah found a wedding dress." Josh turned, leaning against the counter, mug in hand as he pointed towards Jeremiah with it. "We want to be married this weekend. If you can do the honours sometime this weekend, that works."

"Wow!" Jeremiah sat back, not really surprised, he found. "Which day? We're moving on Saturday, but the furniture is already there. It's just what personal stuff we have here."

"And you'd be there now if it wasn't for Leah's situation. Saturday afternoon would work. Just a small ceremony is what she wants. She's really missing her parents."

"And she needs someone to walk her to you." Josh looked up as his father pulled out another chair and sat as well. "I'll do it, Josh. I'll be her father after you two wed. Let me do this for her now."

Josh nodded, for a moment unable to speak. "Thanks, Dad." His voice was husky with emotion.

"But what is this I hear about what happened to you two? I just caught part of it as I was coming in. I wasn't meaning to eavesdrop."

"I know you weren't. Someone tried to ram us from behind. At least I think that was their intent. I had a feeling all the time we were at dinner and then shopping that we were being watched and followed."

Andrew nodded. "I can see that." He looked over his shoulder as he heard the excitement in his wife and daughter's voices, as well as the excited chatter of the little girls. "What about a meal afterwards, Josh?"

Josh sighed. "I'm not good at this planning stuff, am I?" He rose, filling a mug of tea for his father, knowing that was his preference in the afternoon. "I wonder if Mary would have time to cater something. I can't ask my staff, not this weekend. It's the tree lighting and they'll be swamped. I've brought in some extra students like other years." He sighed as he sat. "But that isn't the real problem. The real problem is keeping Leah safe."

Saturday afternoon came quicker than anyone had planned. A scurry of activity had happened, with Leah totally overwhelmed with the love and support she was given, not just by Josh's own family, but by his friends and their families. Mary had gladly offered, without being asked, to prepare a meal for them, hugging Leah as she protested, stating that Josh had been there when Finn and Jacob had needed him the year before, and this was the least she could do.

Leah finally stood in the hallway of the rambling house Andrew and Martha had chosen to live in. She paced, knowing that soon her life would change, but just how much, she really hadn't an idea. She didn't know that the man had set up outside and was waiting for her to emerge on her own, ready to take her captive and disappear with her.

Andrew watched as Martha fussed over Leah, knowing his wife's heart was breaking for Leah, not having her own parents there. Martha's mother had been gone by the time Andrew and Martha had married, taken too soon by heart disease, and she knew just how much a mother was missed. Leah had refused to let her foster family come, despite their asking, stating it was too unsafe for that.

Martha finally hugged Leah and walked away to where Simon was waiting to escort her to a seat. The ladies had decorated the living room for Christmas and large pots of fresh flowers sat around as well.

Andrew approached Leah, waiting until she looked up at him, uncertainty in her eyes.

"Leah, welcome to our family. We're noisy and loud at times, as you know, but you're bringing a peace to it that we need. Josh and you make a great couple, a great team. No matter how you two met, it was already designed by God. Never forget that. He's brought you together." He reached to kiss her cheek, a thumb flicking away a tear as he would have done for his own daughter. "I am privileged now to have two daughters, whom I love immensely. Now, let's get you to Josh."

She nodded, still hesitating. "But Andrew, I bring danger with me. I don't want anyone hurt because of me."

"No, the danger is there, not necessarily because of you. We don't know who or why or what, but I suspect it goes back a long time before you were born."

She finally reached to tuck her hand into the crook of his arm. "Okay, then. Thank you, Andrew."

"Call me Dad if you want. I'd like that, but only when you're ready to do so."

She looked up at him, wonder on her face. "I can't remember calling anyone just Dad. I don't remember my own father well enough to know what I called him, and my foster father was always called by his first name with Dad in front of it."

Josh turned as he heard footsteps and stopped at the beauty of his bride. He knew they were rushing it and he felt remorse at that, but knew from what they had discussed that this was the one way they could think of to keep her safe.

Leah wandered Josh's house when they returned, suddenly at a loss. They were alone for the first time there, and she didn't know what to do. She returned to the kitchen, opening the fridge to place the food Mary had sent home with them on the shelves, before she shut the door and then stood, staring out the window. She could hear Josh on the phone with Amy, checking in to hear how the day had been. Amy had dropped in for the ceremony before heading back to the restaurant.

Josh stopped just before the kitchen door, his eyes watchful as Leah moved restlessly around the kitchen. He regretted rushing her into this, not having had the time, he felt, to properly court her as his grandmother would have said. That he really regretted, he decided, and made a vow to make up for it the rest of the married life. He dropped his eyes to the paper he held, found in his mail from yesterday that he hadn't gotten to. He had spoken with Simon and promised to bring it with him tomorrow to church.

Leah turned, spying him in the hallway and walking towards him, stopping as she saw the paper in his hands.

"Another threat, Josh? What this time?"

He looked up, compassion in his glance as he studied her face. "Another one, Leah. It shouldn't be happening. I want this guy and want him yesterday. He was outside Dad and Mom's house yesterday when we were there. This time he sent a picture of you and Joy's girls."

"The girls?" Her hands flew to her mouth as horror struck her. "He won't go after them, will he?"

"Not if we can help it. I've warned Jeremiah and Joy and also Mom and Dad. They'll watch out for them." He signed, his hand reaching out, waiting until she clasped his hand before he led her to the living room and seated her on the couch, sitting beside her, his eyes on the snapping flames in the fireplace. "We need to figure out who this is. Have you thought of anyone at all, Leah? Anyone else who made you uncomfortable or feel frightened?"

She turned from him for a moment, lost in thought, before she turned back. "On my last job, the one I left to come here, there was one man, older than me, I think around your father's age. I never felt comfortable around him. He wanted me to go out with him, but I always refused. He watched me constantly, to the point I had someone walk me out every day. He left just about a week before I did. I never heard why, but I know the manager was talking to him. There had been complaints about him, what complaints I never heard." She looked up at Josh, who was watching her intently. "His is the voice I heard that day, Josh. Is he from this town?"

Josh shook his head. "No. That was Donald you heard. He lived here for about five years, leaving last year after he duped Blackie and Julia into heading out on a rescue and then we think was part of running them off a cliff." He paused, not quite sure how to continue.

"If you're asking, he was only with our company for less than a year. That goes with what you've said, doesn't it?"

"It does. What name did he go by?"

"Not the name on the list. The first name, yes, but not the last name. I don't know if I ever heard it said. This doesn't make sense, does it? The voice I heard was younger."

"I'll pass that on to Simon and to the chief. Let me have the contact information for the company as well." Josh sighed as he sat back, stretching out his legs in front of him, content for the moment. "Are you up for church in the morning, Leah? We can skip if it you need to."

She stared at him, dumbfounded that he would even ask. "No, we need to be there. It's Jeremiah's first Sunday and we need to support him and Joy."

"They'd understand." He watched as she picked up a cushion and held it against her as she curled up in a corner of the couch. He could see her relaxing as she sat there, her eyes on the fire now. Lord, bless us, please. I know for sure Your hand was in this. Don't let us go wrong, please, dear Lord? Protect my lady.

Chapter 15

Jitting beside Josh the next morning for the service, Leah had interested and some questioning looks sent her way and edged closer to Josh without knowing she was.   Josh reached an arm around her, resting it along the pew back, just touching her shoulders, not realizing that he had just told the whole church she was his. Not that it mattered anyway. He wanted the world to know.

Leah shivered, her eyes going around. She could feel him somewhere in the church. She knew he was there, waiting for an opportunity to take her away from Josh.

She lifted Holly to her knee as the little girl patted her leg, her arms hugging her back against her as the little one leaned on her, watching her sister carefully as she waited for her Uncle Josh to pick her up, finally giving on that and just climbing up on him, his free arm coming around her to hold her steady. He caught Leah's look and grinned.

Then he sobered as he shot a look around. Yes, he felt those eyes, the eyes that both Jacob and Blackie had said they had felt. Whoever it was, he was here. He shifted slightly, watching around them, not seeing anyone in particular.

He caught Leah's look at him and nodded, seeing her sigh and look of distress before Holly asked her something, drawing her attention back to the little girl and then the service.

Josh stood after the service, his arm around Leah as he held her close to him, not wanting her far away, as he stood and talked with different people from the town, introducing Leah as his wife to their surprised looks, but welcoming words.

He raised his eyes at last, catching sight of Donald as he stood, hatred emanating from him as he watched Leah. Josh turned his body slightly, moving between Donald and Leah, catching Jacob's eye and nodding towards the other man. Jacob whispered quickly to Finn and then moved away, his eyes on Donald.

Leah caught the look between the two friends and peeked around Josh, seeing Donald standing there.

"He's here, Josh."

He could hear the fear in her voice. "He is. Jacob's heading his way and I know Simon and Blackie are as well. We'll let them deal with it. Now, Mary has asked if we'd like to come for lunch with them. She has a buffet going on for her clients and says we're more than welcome."

Leah looked down as her hand was clutched tight, seeing the pleading look on Heidi's face.

"Aunt Leah, please come!"

Leah stopped, her words of refusal choking in her throat. She realized that she was an aunt now, with two little ones she could love without reserve. She crouched down as Heidi's arms hugged her tight. "How can I say no, Heidi? We'll come, at least for a while. Does that suit you?"

Heidi's head bobbed up and down in her glee before she was away, looking for her mother. Leah raised up to a standing position, blinking back tears.

"Leah?" Josh was worried, not quite sure what had just happened.

Leah surprised him by hugging him, his own arms going around her. "She called me Aunt. I just realized I have two little nieces."

"That you do. We need to talk at some point, Leah, about where we want to go. No pressure right now. Our priority is keeping you safe." His voice was low enough that only she heard him as he watched while her eyes slid closed, knowing he had just taken off pressure she had put on herself. "As I said, no pressure, Leah. When or if God wills we have a true marriage, we'll know. Right now, I'm just glad you're mine." He tucked her hand into the crook of his elbow and headed out, determined to make the most of the day, knowing that they'd be back at work early the next day, and the next few weeks would be overwhelming for her as she helped in the restaurant office.

Josh stood watching the women laugh and joke around as they were setting up the buffet, Leah among them, a smile on her face. He was taken aback once more at her beauty. He turned his head to look over his shoulder as he heard footsteps approaching from behind him. Jacob and Blackie walked towards him.

"Josh? We need to talk." Blackie motioned towards Timothy's study. Finn's father had told them to use it whenever they needed to.

Josh perched on the arm of the sofa, as Mary called it, watching Blackie, Jacob and Simon as they settled into seats. He understood that Donald had disappeared before Jacob reached him, and no one could tell them where he was.

"You didn't find him today?" Josh's question was more of a statement.

Jacob shook his head. "We didn't, and we couldn't find anyone who saw where he went. He would have been held on to if some of the men had seen him, I can guarantee you that. They want to talk to him about last year."

Josh nodded. "Then I guess it's time I told you that I had another letter come, this time to the house, and this time with photos from yesterday. He's following us wherever we go."

Simon reached for the envelope Josh pulled from his shirt pocket. "I don't like this, Josh. We can't be everywhere you two are."

"Leah doesn't know about this, not yet. I'll have to tell her. I didn't have time yet this morning since I found it." Josh stared down at the floor. "How do we catch him, Simon?"

"That's a good question, Josh. He seems to know where you two are at all times." He frowned. "I'll be right back."

He returned, a small object in his hand, his face grim.

"Is that what I think it is?" Blackie rose and came to study the object.

"It is. A tracker of some kind. That's how they knew you were out of town, Josh." He frowned, a puzzled look coming over his face. "Just what do they want with Leah? She's not from here, had no knowledge of her ancestry."

Josh frowned as well. "That's what I don't get. She did say she had had to be escorted to her vehicle before she left her last job, Donald causing her that much distress."

The men started as they heard a feminine voice in their midst.

"Simon, what is that thing?" Leah pointed to his hand.

"A tracking device I pulled off Josh's vehicle. This is how they've been following you."

She moved closer, her head bent over Simon's hand. "I've seen something like that before. Someone had it on their desk where I worked." She shook her head at Josh's question. "No, not Donald. Someone else. I can't think of who right at the moment, but it will come to me." She studied it closer. "It's the same one. See that little bit of red paint? It's in the same spot as the one I saw." Her gaze was frightened as she raised it to Simon, and then Josh. "Is Donald not the one after me?"

"We think he is, but this changes it all." Simon nodded at Josh's questioning look. "Josh found an envelope in the mail box this morning, Leah. Pictures of you two from yesterday."

She looked up at Simon before she nodded. "Of course, they would do that, now wouldn't they? I'm sorry. They will not scare me with that. It will take a whole lot more than that now." She turned to stare at Josh, reading his support in his eyes before she spoke again. "No matter what happens, they will not break me. Jacob, Finn mentioned that she needed your help in getting something from the storage shed. Simon, here, distracted me from the purpose of telling you when I entered this room for." With a pretended sniff of disdain, she spun on her heel and walked away, leaving the men staring after her before Josh began to laugh and then rose, heading after his wife.

Blackie stared at him, then at the other men. "Is that our Josh?"

"It is, Blackie. He has it bad, I'd say, and so does she. They just haven't come to that conclusion together yet, but they will." Jacob walked away to find his own wife, knowing exactly what she needed from the shelves in the storage shed, the Christmas box of platters and tableware.

Josh drew Leah aside from the buffet line and sheltered her from the rest of the group for a few minutes.

"Are you okay?" He was concerned, seeing the shadow in her eyes.

"I will be." She looked up at him, wondering how she had managed to find a husband so tall, not what she had ever dreamed about, that was for sure. "It's just disheartening, Josh, to have our day spoiled like that."

He ran a finger down her cheek before his hand rested on her shoulder, the finger on her jaw. "I know, sweetheart. I hate that, too. We'll catch him. It's only a matter of time. But are you okay here with everyone? If you're not, we can make our excuses and leave."

She stared at him, not quite sure that she had heard him right. "You'd leave, just for me?"

"I would. You're the most important one in my life now. Always will be. That's a promise I won't break. I may come close but please remind me if I do. We need to come up with a code word for that." He grinned as she smiled and shook a finger at him. "All right, then. If you're sure, then let's get some food before my friends eat it all. Mary's a fantastic cook."

Chapter 16

Late the next afternoon, Josh grabbed the bags of garbage that had been set near the back door and headed outside. He knew Leah was tucked away in his office, finishing off the paperwork that had accumulated over the last few weeks. The restaurant was that busy he had to be in the kitchen a lot of the time, which he loved. Paperwork, he thought, now that I hate. He lifted the lid of the dumpster and tossed the bags in, hearing the lid bang back down. The noise of the lid clanging covered the rushed footsteps heading his way and he heard nothing until he felt something slam into his back, throwing him forward into the dumpster, his head crashing into it.

He dropped to his knees, one hand reaching for his head, the other for his back, even as another blow struck him violently in the ribs sending him once more into the corner of the dumpster and then to the ground. He didn't feel the kick lodged into the same ribs or feel the snap as they broke.

His assailant looked around and hearing noise, ducked behind the bin, waiting.   He knew Leah would come looking for Josh, it was just a matter of time. He shrugged his coat collar up around his ears, pulling his knitted hat down further and glanced up as the snow started falling. Good, he thought. This makes it even better. It will hide my tracks.

The snow continued to fall, gently covering Josh's body even as he lay, unaware of what was happening around him. Blood trickled from his mouth, freezing finally as it dripped to the ground.

Leah paused in the kitchen doorway, searching for Josh and not seeing him. She had a question about some paperwork she had found, paperwork that disturbed her. It had nothing to do with the restaurant but everything to do with her. She knew it hadn't been there the last time she was in the office as she had cleared off his desk of the most current papers.

"Amy?" As Amy turned, Leah headed her way, weaving among the kitchen staff frantically preparing the meals for their customers. "Have you seen Josh?"

Amy paused, a plate in hand that she handed off to another worker before wiping her hands on a towel and tossing that over her shoulder. "He was here ten minutes ago." She looked around. "He's taken the garbage out. But that doesn't take ten minutes."

Leah stared at her, horror and fear running through her before she ran for the door, slamming it open and then stopping to peer around. The snow had covered Josh's tracks, but she headed for the dumpster, her eyes searching in the dimming light. She stumbled as she caught her foot, catching her balance on the metalbin. She looked down and then dropped to her knees, her hands reaching for Josh as she found him at her feet, her hands frantically feeling his back and then his arm for a heartbeat, brushing at the snow that partially covered him. She breathed a sigh of relief as she felt a faint one.

Her calls and then screams for Amy had Amy out the back door of the restaurant, her eyes searching for Leah, searching for

Josh, seeing Leah on her knees and had her starting towards her.

"Amy. An ambulance. Josh is hurt." Leah watched as Amy nodded, her hand opening the back door to call in before she headed across the parking lot, intent on staying with Leah, shrugging into her own jacket, Josh's in her hands to wrap around Leah.

Leah didn't feel the fingers that brushed the back of her sweater as she turned back to Josh, didn't see the dark form slink backwards behind the dumpster as Amy dropped down beside Leah.

"Is he alive?"

"He is, but he's hurt. I can't tell from where though." Leah's worry was palpable. She just knew it was because of her that Josh was hurt, wasn't it? Lord, don't let him die, please, was her cry. Her hands felt through his soaked hair, trying to find a wound on his head, finding nothing. Why was he unconscious? Her worry and fear became palpable. Please, Lord, was her silent cry.

Leah fought against the paramedics and the police officers as they tried to prevent her from riding with Josh. She spun, anger spewing from her, informing them that she was going with him, he was her husband after all. What would they expect her to do?

Chief Waters had approached, listening with a faint smile as the vehement way Leah defended her choice. He finally spoke a quiet word and all resistance dropped. He knew the easier way to keep them both safe was to keep them together.

Leah shot him a look of thanks, then clambered into the rig, finding a seat in a corner, her eyes glued to Josh. She could tell the men were concerned, and so was she.

Leah stood at the head of the stretcher, her eyes on Josh as the medical personnel worked around him, assessing his wounds, running IV lines, preparing him for imaging studies. She refused to move, even when a security officer approached her at a nurse's request. She turned to glare at him, shaking her head, her hand clamped around the stretcher's side rail.

Doc, a friend from church, finally shook his head and told them to let her be, she was fine where she was. He stood back and watched her as the stretcher carrying Josh was wheeled from the examination room, heading for the imagining department. He sighed. Josh, do you know how much this lady loves you? I sure hope you love her that much back.

He headed for the waiting room, knowing Jeremiah and Joy were there and suspecting that Andrew and Martha were as well. He needed someone with Leah and he knew they were the only family she had.

Andrew rose as he saw Doc approaching them, worry on his face.

"Doc?"

"No news yet, Andrew. He's off for some imaging. But I need someone with Leah. She's refusing to move from the examination room, just stands there focused on the door right now. Martha?"

She nodded as she headed back to the room Leah was waiting in. She stood for a moment, her eyes full of compassion on her new daughter. No in law about, she thought.

I know she has Josh's heart and he has hers by the looks of it.

"Leah?" Martha's arm came around the younger woman but she found she could not move her. "Leah? Listen, love. Come and sit. He'll be a while."

Leah finally tore her eyes from the door, a tortured look in them. "It's because of me he's hurt, Martha. It's all my fault."

Martha stared at her, dumbfounded for a moment, before she wrapped her arms around Leah. Leah resisted her hug as much as she could before Martha began to pray for her. As the words washed over her, Leah relaxed, Martha heard the suppressed sobs as Leah wept.

Leah still refused to move from her spot. "I need to be here, Martha. I need to be where Josh can find me."

"That's okay, Leah. Just sit in this chair right here. He can see you right there. They'll likely take him to a room soon, anyway." Martha finally convinced Leah to sit, but Leah didn't stay still.

Leah kept shifting in her chair, her eyes on the door, waiting for Josh to come back, waiting for what she just wasn't sure.

Martha stared at the back of Leah's sweater for a moment, perplexed at the mark, before she drew a deep breath and headed for the waiting room. Finding both her husband and Ed, she drew them back to the room, pointing at Leah's sweater.

"Leah?" When she looked up at Ed, she frowned.

"What is it, Chief? Did you find the person?"

"No, but I need to see your sweater. Do you have another top on under it or can we get you one?"

She shrugged before she pulled off the sweater, revealing a V-neck sweater underneath it and handed it to Ed. He threw a quick glance at her even as he studied the sweater back.

"Leah, I need you to think very carefully. When you first got to Josh, did you see anyone around?"

Leah shook her head. "I don't know. I was just focused on him. Why?"

"Because there's some blood on the back of your sweater and it isn't yours. And where it is couldn't have come from Josh."

She paled as she realized what he was saying. "He touched me? He was that close?"

Ed nodded, compassion in his glance. "He was, Leah. You didn't feel or see anything?"

She shook her head, fear on her face. "Nothing. I was just so focused on Josh." She turned to Martha, who stood, arm around Leah's shoulder. "What have I done, Martha?"

"You have done nothing, child. Nothing at all."

Leah spun on her chair as she heard the stretcher coming back and was on her feet at Josh's side before they had even totally placed it back in its spot. Her eyes were glued to his face even as she reached for his hand. She felt Martha beside her, Martha's own hand covering the younger couple's.

"God is here, Leah. He hears your prayers. Trust him."

Leah finally nodded, knowing that was all she had left. She had to trust.

She struggled to release her hand from under Martha's, only to place it on Josh's cheek, her eyes sad as she saw the bruising. I hate this, Lord, she thought. I hate that he was hurt because of me. Why? Tears sparkled in her eyes and on her lashes, tears she refused to let fall.

Martha stood back, her eye on her son, even as she felt Andrew come to a stop near her, his eyes on his son.

"What have they said, Leah?"

She turned, shaking her head. "Nothing as of yet. The nurse said they were waiting for results and that the doctor would be in shortly." She looked back at Josh, her finger lightly tracing the bruising. "Find who did this, Andrew, please. Find him before he kills one of us. That is his intent. I have no idea who it is or if he is even someone I know. Please?"

He nodded, his head turning as he heard footsteps approaching. Doc stood for a moment, chart in hand, studying the notes, before he looked up, watching Leah as she stood. He knew he needed her to leave, to go home and rest, but he also knew that would be a losing battle. The nurses on the floor would just have to accept the fact that she was not leaving and that he would let her stay.

$\mathcal{D}$uring the early morning hours, Josh began to stir, his eyes finally staying open as he grimaced in his pain, his hand finding the ribs that had been fractured. He gave a low groan, not knowing where he was for a moment. He looked around, squinting as he became accustomed to the low lighting. A hospital room, he thought. Now, why? What happened, Lord, to put me here? I don't remember. All I know is that my back, ribs and head hurt.

He reached carefully to brush at his face, wondering what he could feel tickling it, and caught a lock of hair. He stared at it. Deep red. Leah?

His head turned slightly and he saw his bride curled up on the bed beside him, a light blanket covering her. He gave a small smile. She was here. She hadn't left, like he thought she would. Love for her flooded through his heart and he know he didn't ever want her to leave. Reaching carefully, he withdrew his arm from between them and snuggled her close to him, her head fitting under his chin. He turned so his cheek rested against her head and he slept again.

He roused somewhat later as he felt a hand on his wrist and looked around. One of the nurses stood there, her eyes watching him as she checked his IV.

"How are you feeling, Josh?" Her voice was low.

"Sore, but not as sore as I will be. What happened?"

She shook her head. "I don't know for sure, but someone said you were attacked outside your restaurant. The chief will be by in the morning."

He nodded, his hand going to his ribs. "What did I do to the ribs?"

"You fractured about three. And you have bruised kidneys. Whoever beat you did a good job." She turned and walked away, not seeing him staring after her before he looked down at Leah.

Why, Lord? I need to keep her safe and I can't if I'm laid up like this. Heal me quickly, please?

Leah stirred in the later hours, her hand coming up to rub at her face before she raised her head at a sound. She stilled, seeing a man standing in the room, his eyes on Josh. She could feel the evil coming from him and froze even more, not wanting to let him know she was awake. She tried to see his face but the shadows hid it. He finally walked away, leaving her breathing a sigh of relief but still scared.

Leah turned her head slightly, studying Josh's face, seeing the bruising on his forehead and cheek. Who did this, she wondered once more. Josh was watching her as she turned, a small smile on his face.

"Leah, hi." He had to clear the early morning huskiness from his voice. "You're here."

"Where else would I be? You're hurt. Of course, I'd be here."

He nodded and regretted it as pain pounded through his head, causing his eyes to slide closed. When he cracked them open again, Leah was sitting up, concern on her face, the nurse coming through the door.

"You called the nurse!"

"Of course I did. You need something for pain." Leah pushed herself away from him and off the bed, starting to pace before she walked from the room. She needed some time to think. Being that close to Josh didn't help. She had to come up with a plan to end this, to find the culprit and bring him to justice.

She stopped as she saw the police chief walking towards her.

"Chief? You're here early." She glanced at her watch.

He smiled. "I know I am. I wanted to talk to both you and Josh before the day got going. Is he awake?"

She nodded, as she turned, her hand coming on to stop Ed as he walked by her. "Do you have news who did this?"

He shook his head. "We're still looking at surveillance videos and trying to find the assailant. Did you see anything that you have remembered?"

"I was too focused on finding Josh. I didn't see or hear anything." She frowned at him. "Why?"

"Because we don't see him leaving. We see the assault on Josh and then he disappears behind the dumpster. We see him reach for you and then disappear. He doesn't show up anywhere."

"What does that mean?" She looked at him horrified. "Is he with the emergency services?"

"That would be one explanation. Another is that he managed to hide behind someone and leave." Ed sighed. "Let's go talk to your fellow and see if he remembers anything."

❄ ❄ ❄ ❄

Josh was moved home three days later, worried about his restaurant, even though Amy told him she had it under control, as much as he was missed, that he needed time to heal. He shook his head at her and finally agreed.

He sank gratefully down into his own bed, nodding at his father's help, the nod almost too much of an effort, and then pulling the covers over himself as he laid back on the pillows. His eyes slid shut from relief. The pain medications were kicking in and he knew he'd be out before long. He wanted desperately to be out there hunting for his assailant but knew he just couldn't.

"Do you need anything, son?" Andrew's voice held the concern he knew he could not speak.

"No, I'm fine. Thanks, Dad. Talk to Leah, please. Let her know it's not her fault." His eyes closed and he slept.

Andrew stood for a moment before he headed to look for Leah, finding her standing in the kitchen, her hand on the fridge door, her eyes on the stove.

"That's an interesting position, Leah. Planning on cooking?"

She shook her head as she looked over at him. "Frankly, I have no idea what I'm doing any more, other than being a danger to Josh."

"Now that we don't know for sure, Leah. It could have been anyone who went after him." He pointed to a chair. "Sit. Josh asked me to talk to you. Do you know why?

She sighed as she pulled out a chair, then turned to reach for the coffee she had poured for them, setting Andrew's down in front of him. "Can I get you anything else?"

Andrew smiled at her, knowing she was putting off the talk they needed to have. "I'm fine, Leah. Sit, please." He waited as she did. "Now, about what happened to Josh. We have no way of knowing who it was and if it was connected to you." He held up a hand as she protested. "It's the truth, Leah. Until the police find whoever it was, we won't know. We can't live our lives as if everyone is out to get us." He watched carefully as she finally relaxed and sat back.

"I know that, Andrew, in my head. It's my heart that I can't convince of that." She shot a look towards the hallway. "Josh was hurt because of me. I just know it."

Andrew shook his head. "Again, Leah. We don't know that for sure. If we did, we'd have you two put somewhere safe." He sipped at his coffee, gathering his thoughts. "Now, about what Josh also wanted me to talk to you about. No, that doesn't make much sense, now does it?"

Leah smiled and reached to pat Andrew's hand. "It made perfect sense. What doesn't make sense is what Josh wanted you to talk to me about."

"Leah, you are a descendent of one of the founding families. You never knew that until the last few days. That may be why someone has targeted you. It may not be." He paused, his eyes seeking the window, before he nodded, having received the words he needed from the Lord. "You do not have to work, ever again. You have buildings you own in this town. Not many but a few. They are rented well and the tenants want to stay. You also have a bank account in your name now." He reached into his pocket and pulled out an envelope. "When you're ready, Josh will take you over to the bank and get it all set up for you. The police chief has spoken to the bank manager and he's just waiting for you to come in."

She stared at him, then at the envelope. "How? Shouldn't someone else get it?"

Andrew shook his head. "No. The town charter is specific. The assets go to the descendants of the families. If there are no descendants, the assets go into a trust and are proportioned out the to remaining families after a certain period of time. Do you understand?" At her nod, he continued. "The assets go to the male heir first and then to the female. It would have gone to your father but because he's not here and you're his heir, it goes to you."

"Wow! That's a lot to take in." Leah stared at him once more, her eyes not blinking. Andrew smiled, thinking she had a "deer in the headlights" look. "This is what Josh wanted you to talk to me about?" She spun to stare at the window behind her, suddenly comfortable, feeling as if someone was standing there watching her. She turned back to Andrew. "What about Josh?"

"I have divided what I received between Joy, Josh and myself. He asked for the restaurant. He was a cook in the armed forces and wanted to make a difference in a town with a new style of restaurant. I think he's done that. He's well loved by all."

"Not by all. I'm sorry, Andrew. Someone doesn't like him very much."

"No, they don't." He looked around as he heard a sound and Josh appeared in the doorway, ragged and weary looking.

Leah rose, her arm going around him as he staggered a bit, drawing him to a chair, her hand resting on his shoulder as she watched him closely.

Andrew studied the two as Josh looked up, nodding his thanks. Thank you, Lord. You've provided just who Josh needs in Leah. A strong woman, who knows what she wants and is willing to fight for it. She won't take anything from anyone when it comes to her family and that's what he needs. He's very much a protector and she needs that in her life. Bless them, Lord.

"Dad? Did you talk with Leah?" Josh's head dropped to his folded arms and his voice was muffled.

Leah shared a look of concern with Andrew, who shook his head.

"I did, son. Now, do you want something to eat? If not, let me help you back to bed. You're almost asleep again on your feet."

Leah finally turned off most of the lights in the house late that night, stopping at Josh's bedroom door before she entered. He was asleep but she could see the pain in his face. She hesitated, finally reaching for a blanket and curling up beside him on the bed. She sighed, knowing that tomorrow was another day and there would be no way she'd be able to keep him from the restaurant. She had to go in any way to do paperwork.

Josh roused as Leah settled beside him, his heart raising in prayer for his bride. Lord, she's hurting in ways I can't fix, only You can. This is where I just have to trust you. Please, Lord? End this soon so we can get on with our lives?

Amy looked at the young couple the next morning as Josh sat on a stool near the counter, his eyes on the paperwork Leah had set in front of him, needing his signatures. His arm had come around her waist and she leaned on his shoulder, pointing out what she needed. Amy shook her head. Yep, she thought.   Another couple in love.   That leaves only Simon, and who could she find for him?

Josh looked up at Leah at that moment, catching her eye and seeing something that gave him hope. She shook her head at him, her eyes going to the staff, before she looked back at him.

"Josh, there's something in the office I think the police need to see. Amy said a parcel was delivered yesterday. I didn't open it. I don't like the looks of it."

He stood, watched as she gathered the paperwork and then swung his arm around her again as she turned to the office. He knew something had spooked her and he wanted to stop that, now. Lord, please! I need to have this stopped. It's slowly killing my bride and I don't like that. Give us strength, please, dear Lord.

He stared at the box, medium sized, wrapped in plain paper with Leah's name and the restaurant address in block print. He reached for his phone even as he sighed. This is not how he planned to spend today, that was a given.

Ed looked at the two and then at the techs as they carefully moved the package. They looked up at him and one spoke quiet enough that the young couple didn't hear what was said. He looked over at them and then spoke, pointing to the box.

The techs took the box as they left, telling Josh and Leah Ed would let them know what was in it. The young couple shared a look before Ed spoke to them.

"I'll follow them to see what they have and then I'll be back. Will you be here or at home?"

Leah spoke. "At home. Josh is at his limit right now."

Josh just stared at her, then began to laugh. "Hen-pecked already, Ed, and that not even after a week." He wrapped Leah in a hug, not letting her see the grimace that came with it, shaking his head slightly at Ed as he went to speak.

Later that night, Leah stepped back from the open door as both Ed and Simon entered, grim looks on their faces. Her eyes shot to where Josh stood in the kitchen doorway.

He pointed to the living room. "Why don't we have a seat in there?" He turned back to kitchen, but Leah was ahead of him, lifting the tray to prevent him from doing so. He stopped her with a hand on her arm, his own eyes studying hers before he dropped a kiss on her cheek and then turned away, not seeing the softening of her face.

Simon took the tray from her and set it down, waiting as she took two mugs and then settled down beside Josh, who reached over and tucked her tight to him, before handing her back her mug. Ed and Simon shared a smile, knowing what they had to say would be difficult for the couple to hear.

Leah finally shared a look with Josh, who took her mug from her, setting it down on the side table, and reaching for her hand. She looked over at Simon and then Ed.

"Ed? Simon?"

The two officers shared a look, before Simon spoke.

"We do have information that really impacts who you are, Leah. I'll let Ed explain what was in the box."

Ed looked down at the folder he had set on the coffee table before he reached for it, his heart sore for what he would have to tell her. *Lord, I need your words. Please speak through me. I'm glad she has Josh right now. He'll get her through this, as sore as he is. He has a strength in him I have seen in few, other than his friends and their families. I know it comes from you.*

"Ed?" Leah's quiet voice broke into his prayer and he looked up, his eyes catching Josh as he looked down at Leah, his heart on his face and in his own eyes.

"Leah. That box was delivered to you and to you only. It has nothing to do with Josh or the restaurant. That doesn't explain how whoever it was knew your married name or where to find you."

"Someone has been watching me very closely, I would say. We already know that."

"That's correct, Leah. Now, as to the contents, I just need to ask a few questions. They're likely questions we've already asked you, but please bear with me. I just need to verify the facts before I go on."

Leah confirmed what Ed asked, a puzzled look on her face, knowing she had already answered those questions before, with both Ed and Simon. She looked at Josh, who was watching her intently, concerned about how it was affecting her.

Ed finally reached for the folder, hesitating before he handed it to her.

"These are photos that the techs took. They are what was contained in the box." He hesitated once more before he handed it to her. "Don't open it yet, please, Leah. This is going to change what you have know about your life. Are you prepared for that?"

She shrugged after pondering his words. "I need to know, Ed. There has always been this question about my life that has never been answered. I know Mom and Dad Whitley wanted to adopt me so badly but were refused every time. That hurt all of us." She reached to open the folder, stopping as Josh's hand covered hers, gripping it tightly. She looked up at him.

"We need to pray first, Leah. If this is as big as Ed says, we need God at the centre. We need His strength." He searched her eyes and face, seeing her agreement, then turned to Simon, who nodded and led them off in a powerful prayer.

Ed finally nodded to the folder. "Open it now, Leah. Look at it very carefully. We have some answers, but not all."

Leah looked at him, apprehension in her eyes before she turned to look at Josh. He nodded to the folder.

"Let's see what we have, Leah."

She slowly opened it, searching through the photos, before she raised her eyes to Ed.

"What does this mean? These are pictures of me over the years."

"They are, Leah. Someone has watched you very carefully. This shows that. What the intent was, we don't know at this point. There is nothing to show us who it has been."

She flipped back through them, pausing at one. "I recognize this one, but who's that in the background? I don't know that person at all. He's so close to us." She passed it back to Simon.

Simon studied it, fear rising in him. If it was who he thought it was, Leah was in more danger than she knew. "I might know who that is, but I need to do some research." He glanced at her.

"Leah, I think Simon needs to talk to you." Josh's quiet words caught her attention.

She looked up at Simon, a frown on her face. "Simon? I thought you were done."

"Sorry, Leah. I'm not. Something has come to our attention, coupled with these photos, that we need to look at." He shared a look with Ed. "Someone has approached our office, asking about a missing child."

She drew in a deep breath. "Me?"

Simon nodded. "It may be. A little three-year-old girl disappeared from the other coast about the same time you appeared in foster care here, about a week to ten days' difference." He reached for his jacket, pulling out a swab kit. "If we can test your DNA, we may be able to link you to that family."

She nodded, then held up a hand. "Is it possible, do you think?"

Simon shared a look with Josh, seeing the worry and hope on Josh's face. "It is, Leah. Let me do the swab and then I have something to show you."

She waited for him to tuck the sample away and then took the folder he handed her, not quite sure what to expect. She just knew it would change her life and she wasn't sure she was ready for that. Her eyes closed as she begged God for strength, for hope, for peace. She felt the folder gently removed from her hands and Josh's arms hugging her tight before a finger traced the tears on her cheeks.

She looked up at him, realizing that she wasn't alone on this journey, that God had provided for her before she even knew what she was facing.

"You open it, Josh. You open it first." She urged him, a pleading look on her face.

"Are you sure?" At her nod, he flipped it open, his hand freezing as he looked at the page with the side-to-side photos. His eyes raised to Simon, who nodded.

"Leah. You need to look at this. But, sweetheart, I need to prepare you." Josh stopped, not sure how to proceed.

"Is it me?" Leah's voice could barely be heard. "It's me, isn't it?"

Josh nodded, sadness on his face. "I think so." He turned the picture to show her and heard her cry of shock and then the sobs. He didn't feel Simon reach for the folder, didn't feel the pain from his ribs and back as he cradled Leah in his arms, his head on hers as she sobbed, her heart broken, her hand fisted in his sweater.

Later, she looked at Simon, meeting his compassionate glance. "Now what, Simon?"

"First, we confirm your DNA. That will take a few weeks, unfortunately. But I will be in touch with the detective who sent this. He's been contacting police services on this side of the country as that had never been done. He's been going back over cold case files and came across yours. He wasn't satisfied with the supposition that you had drowned in a creek in your town. That's what everyone thinks because they found your blanket on the bank and one of your shoes in the water. But the woman who was to have been watching you disappeared the same day you did, and no one has ever been able to find her to question her. There has always been a question in everyone's mind if she took you and left evidence to the contrary." His paused, working to quell his anger. "Your mother has never lost hope that you are still alive and that she'll see you once more. You were their only child. They could have no more."

Leah's tears flowed once more at that. "How cruel!"

Josh held her tight once more, sharing a look with first Simon and then Ed. "How fast can we get confirmation? Do we have to wait for confirmation or can we meet her parents?"

Simon paused, having considered just that. "What I would suggest is that you let either Ed or I contact the detective out there, get his feelings and then go from there. I'm sure the couple would want to come here as soon as possible. But with Leah in danger as she is, we don't want to place anyone else in the line of fire to say the least."

"I think I would want to wait, Simon. Wait for confirmation. I don't want to get their hopes up for nothing. I mean. I know I look like that little girl, our pictures are so similar, but it would be cruel to do this to them. Besides, as you say, we need to solve who it is after me first before I can go on with anything else. And how close are you to that?"

Simon shared another look with Ed and then Josh, finding both men nodding in agreement with Leah. "That's what we'll do then, Leah. I'll get the sample to the lab in the morning. With the possibility of you being the missing child, that will expedite it. I know the couple placed DNA on file a few years ago, so that will help."

Josh turned back from locking the doors after the two men, searching for Leah, finding her in the kitchen cleaning away their coffee mugs and preparing the room for the morning. He paused, leaning against the door jamb.

"Leah?"

She turned, and he saw the fatigue and fear and yet hope on her face. "Do you think it's them, Josh? Will I finally find my family? It's not that the Whitleys weren't family, but they're not blood, and I've always felt that I was missing someone."

He walked towards her, his hands coming to rest on her upper arms. "I think they are but we need to pray hard about this. This will be a shock for them, and I know they'll want to see you right away."

She nodded, then yawned. "You need to be in bed, Josh. Did you get your pain meds?"

"I did, thank you. Head off. I'll make sure everything's locked up and the lights are off." He stopped her as she went to walk past him to drop a kiss on her cheek before he headed for the back door, not seeing the look of surprise she gave him.

Chapter 18

Three months passed without Ed or Simon any closer to finding the person responsible for sending the box to Leah or who had assaulted Josh. They were growing frustrated but there was not a lot they could do about that.

Josh watched as Leah grew white and thin. He hated this for her but knew he could do nothing, except pray. His family joined him in that.

He looked up one day as Simon entered the restaurant office, an official envelope in hand.

"Simon?"

"Is Leah around, Josh?" Simon had some news. He hadn't looked at the results but the tech had handed them to him, a small smile on her face as she did so. Simon had talked to Leah the day before, letting her know he had the results, hadn't seen them, but was given to understand by the tech that they were what they had all suspected.

"She's just down the street at Finn's." Josh looked down at his desk and then rose. "This can wait. Leah wanted some signatures and I'm about done."

Simon dropped into a chair. "Finish this off. I doubt you'll be back today."

Josh's hand froze as he reached for his pen, his eyes on Simon. "Is it good news?"

"I have no idea. Not for sure. Either way, Leah will need you today and that should be away from here. If it's a celebration, take her out somewhere for dinner."

Josh nodded, then quickly scrawled his signature on the cheques. Simon reached for them and folded the copies of the invoices and the cheques into the envelopes Leah had already prepared, stacking them neatly before handing them to Josh.

"Drop these in the mail box on the way by and you can tell Leah you finished the task she assigned you." Simon laughed at the look Josh shot him before Josh rose, grabbing his jacket and the envelopes, calling out to Amy that he was gone for the day.

Finn turned as the door opened and the two men entered, shooting a quick look behind them.

"Afternoon, Finn. How are you this fine day?" Simon grinned as she shook a finger at him.

"I'm fine, Simon, but a little confused. Leah left to go back to the restaurant a good thirty minutes, Josh. Did she not make it there?" Concern coloured Finn's face.

Josh shook his head before turning back to the door. He stopped before he spun to face Finn. "Did she say if she planned to stop anywhere between here and there?"

Finn hesitated, then shrugged. "Not that I know of, Josh. She seemed extra happy this morning, as if she had a secret she wanted to share but couldn't."

Josh just grinned at her prying comment. "She was, was she? I'll have to ask her about that when I track her down."

Finn sputtered out words as Josh walked through the door, before she turned to Simon, her words halting as she saw the look on Simon's face and began to fear the worst.

Simon watched Josh as he headed back for the restaurant, disturbed that Leah wasn't at either place.

"Finn? Can you call Blackie for me and have him meet me at the restaurant?" He walked away, not catching her quick glance of concern.

Simon caught up with Josh as he stared around the kitchen of the restaurant, having searched for Leah in the whole building.

"She's not here, Simon. Where is she?"

"Would she have stopped anywhere?"

Josh shrugged, then reached for his phone, walking away from Simon for a moment. He had called their physician's office, knowing that Leah wanted to make an appointment and he prayed that she was there. He turned back to Simon, worry on his face.

"Not where you thought she'd be?" Simon was worried as well, just not wanting to let Josh know that.

"No. She wanted to see the doctor but her appointment isn't until later today." He paced, then headed for the door. "I'm going store to store, Simon. I don't like the feeling I'm getting. Amy, if Leah shows up, have her call me."

Simon took one side of the street as Josh walked the other side, finally meeting up together near the town square. No one had seen Leah since before she had been at Finn's.

"Now what, Simon? Where do we search?" Josh turned in a circle, desperately seeking any sign of Leah.

"I've called Ed. He's sending officers to start searching buildings around the centre of town, working their way out. We'll find her, Josh."

Josh nodded, fear and concern in his heart. He prayed as he didn't think he had prayed before, asking for Leah to come home safely. He walked away from Simon, his eyes seeking his wife, not finding her.

Early evening found Josh in his kitchen, hands jammed into his jeans pockets, not listening to the quiet conversation going on around him, his eyes on Ed and the officers setting up equipment in his living room, just in case a ransom call came in. His mother approached him, but he just shook his head. She stopped, then retreated, Andrew's arm finding its way around her shoulders.

"Let him be, love. He's hurting and he doesn't know how to react right now." Andrew looked over at Jeremiah who nodded his agreement. Joy stood near her brother, wanting to help him but not knowing how, other than to be close. Their two girls were with Finn's parents.

Ed stood quickly from where he was seated, walking away as he pulled out his phone. He spun, his eyes seeking Josh, as relief washed over his face. He pocketed his phone, spoke quietly to the officers, who nodded, and then approached Josh.

Josh had watched Ed take his call and turn to find him. He waited for Ed to speak, but Ed didn't seem to be able to find the words.

"You found her?" At Ed's nod, relief coursed through him, then fear. "She's alive?"

"She is, Josh. She's hurt but they're transporting her to the hospital now. Let's get you there. I'll leave the officers here for now, just in case any calls come through." He looked past Josh at Josh's family, who were scurrying to find their coats. Jeremiah shoved Josh's into his hands, but Josh made no effort to put it on, clutching it tight instead as he headed for the door.

Jeremiah's hand on his arm stopped him. "Let me drive you, Josh."

Josh finally nodded and headed for that vehicle, sliding into the back seat as Joy fastened her seat belt.

Josh almost ran through the doors of the Emergency Department, heading for the desk, desperate to find Leah. The clerk smiled compassionately at him as she asked him to have a seat. She would let the physician know he was here, that Leah was being assessed at the moment. He hesitated before nodding, pleading that they let him go back as soon as they could.

He turned and paced, not seeing his friends come through the door, not seeing the officers Ed had asked to be there for his protection. He didn't see his mother and sister sitting watching him, fear on their faces. His father stood near the door, his eyes flickering between Josh, the door to the examination rooms and the rest of his family and their friends. Jeremiah paced with him, knowing that Josh just needed someone to stand with him, that no conversation was necessary.

It seemed hours later to Josh that the door finally opened and the physician walked towards him. He drew a breath of relief, seeing it was Doc. He approached, stopping suddenly in fear. He couldn't read Doc's face and felt his heart sinking in his chest. How bad was she?

"Doc?" He reached to shake the hand Doc held out.

"Josh. We need to stop meeting like this, you know. Between you and your friends, this is becoming a habit." He gave a small grin as Josh shook his head at him. His eyes saw Josh's family moving to stand behind him.

"Doc?"

"She's okay, Josh. Battered and bruised and very cold but she's fine."

"Did she say what happened?" Josh's brow wrinkled as he puzzled through what Doc had said.

"Not really, other than that she was running down some stairs and tripped and fell." At Josh's quickly indrawn breath, Doc's hand went up. "She slid down about seven stairs. Her back is bruised. She has a hairline fracture in her tibia from the way she landed at the bottom of the stairs. She was there for a few hours before she was found and is very cold and in pain. We're working on warming her up. She's refusing pain medications. She says she won't take them. Maybe you can talk to her and see if you can convince her she needs them." He paused, a slight smile on his face, as he watched Josh take in what he had said.

Josh's eyes slid closed and his heart raised in praise that she wasn't hurt worse. It could have been so much worse. Then, his eyes popped open and he stared at Doc, seeing the slight smile on his face.

"Doc?" When Doc didn't answer, Josh moved closer to him, not realizing how close his family was to him. "The baby?" His voice was low, trying to keep that fact confidential until he saw Leah and he reassured himself both were fine. They had decided not to tell their family or friends yet. It was just too new to them.

Doc's smile widened a bit. "Both are fine. The way Leah made herself fall protected the little one. Come on. Let's get you back to her. We do have a fetal monitor on for now." His voice was equally quiet. Doc was reading Josh's stance and knew he wanted that fact kept quiet but he didn't think it had worked, not by the looks on the faces behind Josh.

Josh walked away, leaving his family staring after him, mouths open.

"Did he just ask about a baby?" Martha turned to Andrew, wonder on her face.

"He did, love. We need to let that go. It's up to them to tell us." He raised his eyes to the rest of them standing there. "Is that understood? He has enough to worry about without any of us asking questions he may not be ready to answer as of yet. If they had known for a while, they would have told us. When they do tell us, we all act as if we knew nothing about it." Andrew nodded towards the exam rooms. "She may still lose it, given what she's been through. We need to let them have this time."

Finn shared a look with Jacob. "That's what I picked up on then today. She was glowing when I saw her earlier." She leaned into her husband's arm. "Please, Lord, don't let them lose it."

Josh stood for a moment just inside the door, watching as the nurse finished her task and then moved away from the bedside, before he approached. He stood by the bedside, his eyes on Leah, watching as she dozed. He searched her face, seeing the pain and fatigue lining it. He reached for her hand, the one she had on the outside of the blankets they were using to warm her body. He rubbed his thumb on the back of it, feeling the chill in her skin, praying that the Lord would warm her quickly.

His eyes raised to the various monitors, stopping as he caught sight of the heartbeat on the fetal monitor, wonder growing within his heart.

He felt his hand squeezed and looked back down at Leah, finding her eyes on him and a faint smile on her face. He laid the back of his fingers against her cheek before he reached to kiss her.

"Hi." Her voice was hoarse.

"Hi, yourself. How are you feeling?"

"Sore. I tried to fall the right way, Josh. I just don't know if I did it right. The doctor said I fractured a leg bone and am bruised." She frowned at him. "I really didn't want to end up bruised like you, you know."

He smiled, reassurance flowing from him that made her relax. "I know you didn't. You'll need to tell me what happened, but not right now. I hear tell you're refusing any pain medication."

She nodded, wincing at the pain. "I am. I just can't, Josh."

"I know, sweetheart." His eyes raised again to the monitor and she followed his line of sight, wonder overcoming her.

"Is that the baby?"

"It is. Doc said the way you fell you protected it." He turned as Doc entered the room, file in hand.

Doc stopped before he reached the bed, a frown on his face, before he looked up, catching their eyes on him. He smiled.

"Everything looks good, Josh. Leah. It doesn't look as if the baby was harmed." He frowned at her. "Now about your pain, young lady."

"I won't take anything. I absolutely refuse." She frowned as Josh began to laugh and Doc grinned, shaking her file at her.

"That's what I thought you said. We plan on keeping you in at least overnight and maybe an extra day, just in case. The obstetrician will be in tomorrow to see you."

He paused, leaning against the end of her bed, crossing his feet. "Do you have any questions at all, either one of you?" When they looked at each other and then shook their heads, he straightened up. "I'll be around for a while if you do. If not, the doctor who's covering for me will be in tomorrow to see you." He shot a look at Josh, not quite sure what to say. "The chief is waiting to speak with you, Leah. Josh, can I have a word?"

Josh looked down at Leah before he nodded, following Doc out of the room.

"Doc? What aren't you saying?"

Doc shook his head. "All is well with Leah. I just thought you should have a head's up that your family may have guessed what's going on. I can't be sure that they do."

Josh sighed. "I figured that out when I looked back at them. I would rather just leave it like it is for now. Leah just told me last night. It's so new we didn't want to say anything yet."

Doc smiled. "From the looks of it, your father was laying down the law." He reached to shake Josh's hand as he saw Ed approaching. "Now, I'm out of here. Call me if you have any concerns."

Ed stood for a moment, his eyes on Josh, seeing the fatigue on the younger man's face and knowing the questions he had to ask would only make it worse.

"Is Leah up to talking with me, Josh?"

Josh looked at the closed door and sighed. "I would rather she wait, but she'll want to do it tonight. Come on, then. The sooner you ask your questions, the sooner I can get her settled."

Chapter 19

Leah stood in their kitchen the night before all what happened to her transpired. She stared down at the water in the sink, her hands gripping the edge of the counter, not quite sure how to approach Josh. What she had to tell him was something they really hadn't talked about, and now she was at a loss for words.

Josh watched his wife for a few minutes before he approached her, wrapping her into his arms, his chin on the top of her head. When she didn't move, he turned her to face him.

"Leah? What's going on? You're quiet tonight, and you hardly touched your dinner. Are you sick?" Concern laced his words.

She shrugged, and he saw the faint glimpse of tears in her eyes. Worried, he scooped her into his arms and headed for their favourite chair in the living room, settling down himself and cradling her close on his knee.

"Talk to me, Leah. What is going on?"

Her head on his shoulder, she gripped his hands tightly for a moment, a habit that she was really trying hard to break, that of gripping hard to something when she was scared or uncertain.

She finally spoke. "You had a good day?"

"I did. And you? You left early today. I missed you at the office."

She nodded. "I know. I had to run an errand." She looked up at him, uncertainty in her glance. "We've talked about so many things over the last few months, Josh, but there is one thing we never really touched on."

He tilted his head to study her face, not quite sure where she was going with her words. "And that would be?"

"A family. We never have talked much about that."

"No, we haven't. I guess I figured that you would want to wait, given what you've been through. I know we're still waiting for the test results to come back and I thought we'd talk once they were back."

"Simon talked to me today. I have the tentative test results and need to talk to you about that. That little girl is me. He said he'd talk to the detective on the coast. He'll bring the official results to us tomorrow." There was sadness in her voice and on her face.

"That's good news, isn't it?" Josh was confused at her reaction.

"It is and it isn't. Mom and Dad Whitley will be hurt. We may never know what transpired though to get me here on this coast."

"God knows, sweetheart." Josh studied her face once more, still confused. "But that's not all. What is all this talk about family?"

She stared at him, the answer in her eyes and on her face.

"Leah? Are you telling me something?" Hope surged within him, that they would be starting a family, sooner than he had thought.

She nodded. "I am, Josh. We're having a baby and I don't know that I'm ready for that."

Josh kissed her soundly and then hugged her tight. "We'll get there."

They sat for a while, conversation quiet and light before Leah finally stood, yawning as she did so, Josh standing as well, heading off to finish the work in the kitchen and then to make sure everything was locked up for the night.

The next day, she thought back to Josh's reaction and smiled, her mind really not on the bookwork she was to be doing. She finally rose, having finished everything, and headed for the kitchen, finding Josh deep in the orders flying into the kitchen. She gave a small wave at Amy as she headed for the door. Josh's birthday was coming up and Finn had called, saying she had just the gift Leah was looking for.

Finn looked up as Leah entered, giving a small wave as she handed a customer the box she had just wrapped, before heading for Leah.

"Leah. Thanks for coming in. This way." Finn led the way back to her office, pointing to the chairs. "Sit. Do you want coffee or something?"

"I'm fine, Finn. Did you get it?"

"I did. It took some time, but here is the cookbook you wanted. It's a first edition too, from the late 1800s. I think he'll like it."

Leah took the book carefully into her hands. "Oh, I think he will." She paged through it, excitement growing within her. "Can I leave it here with you until the weekend? I don't know where I would hide it at home. Josh is wanting to change some rooms around."

"Not a problem, Leah. Any word on the DNA results?" Finn knew it had been months and that Leah was getting anxious for the answers, that she needed them in order to move on with her life.

She shook her head. "Simon has them and I've talked to him." She stared at Finn and then started to laugh at the disgruntled look on Finn's face. "Don't worry. Once Josh and I have discussed them, I'll tell you." She glanced at her watch. "I need to run. I have an appointment later this afternoon, and I need to head home for a bit. Thanks again, Finn, for finding this book." She hugged Finn and headed for the door, not looking back, not seeing the puzzled look on Finn's face, who had picked up on something about her friend.

Leah stood for a moment, her face raised to the sky, praise and thanksgiving flowing to her Father in heaven. Josh had taken her news, both parts, well, and that morning was already planning how to turn a room downstairs into a nursery. She had laughed at him, telling him they had months yet to do just that. He had replied that he knew that, he was just dreaming, even as he wrapped her into his arms, his strength comforting in a way she had not felt before.

She didn't hear the heavy footsteps that approached her as she stood in front of the alleyway, lost in thought. She was suddenly wrapped into an iron arm, a hand clasped across her mouth to muffle her cries for help. She was still for a second, then began to fight desperately, wanting to get loose and unable to do just that. She was half-walked, half-carried down the alleyway, her captor searching the area around him. He stopped, turning his body so she was shielded for any eyes that might see them. He then dragged her forward, a warning growled into her ear that if she screamed, Josh would be hurt. He had someone in the restaurant, watching him.

She nodded, fighting back the tears that clouded her vision. She couldn't get a look at the man, not the way he held her, but she knew he wasn't much taller than her and heavyset. She felt his arm loosen from around her and she turned, ready to flee, only to have her upper arm caught into an iron fist and she was dragged along the back streets. She desperately looked for help and saw no one. It was close to lunchtime and everyone was off the streets.

She was shoved into a building and then into a room where she was pushed hard down into a chair. The man paced, his voice rumbling away as he muttered to himself. She finally looked up and froze. No, she thought. Please, God! Not this man! I need Your help to get away. I know I can't do it on my own.

The man turned, his eyes hard on her as she stared back at him before he gave a cruel grin.

She shrank back against the chair, not sure what he had planned, but knowing it was not in her best interest.

"So, Leah. At last I have you where I want you. You'll not get away from me." The man stood in front of her, arms crossed against his ample belly.

"Duane. I should have known it was you. I always knew there was something evil about you."

"Evil?" His voice rose in a scream. "There is nothing evil about me. You should know better." His hand reached out to slap her. Then he stopped. "No, I can't hit you. I can't damage your face."

Leah continued to stare at him, her face blank, her mind racing as she tried to think of a way to get away from him. He was the one person she had prayed never to see again. He had haunted her working days at her last job, trying to get her to go for lunch or dinner, always hanging around when she went to leave, to the point that she always asked someone to walk her to her car. She had spurned the advances, or what she thought were advances, from a man old enough to be her father.

Duane Alberts stormed around the room, his voice echoing from the walls as he talked to himself, his words liberally laced with profanity. He would turn at odd moments, his eyes fastening on Leah as she sat, her eyes on the floor in front of her, her hands folded on her lap, calm and peace flowing from her in contrast to his rage. She listened as he detailed every attempt on their lives, every assault, every package, every envelope that they had received. All from him, and with the express purpose of driving them apart and terrorizing them.

He stormed over to stand in front of her, ready to speak, numerous times before he would step away and begin to pace once more. Leah kept an eye on him, not sure what he had planned or when he would let her go. She was afraid to move, afraid that he was right and someone was watching Josh and would harm him if she disobeyed Duane's commands. Her feet were starting to chill from the cement floor and she knew it was only a matter of time before the chill spread through her whole body, and that she wanted to avoid.

She shuddered as she heard a new voice behind her. Donald. How did he fit into this?

"Dad? What have you done?"

"Donald! What are you doing here? I told you to watch Josh."

"Well, guess what. He's left the restaurant, searching for her." He nodded at Leah. "I can't keep track of him any more, so I came here. What have you done?"

"What have I done?" Duane's voice rose in a screech. "What do you mean, what have I done?"

"Yes, that's what I said. What have you done? Why is Leah here?" He pointed to her. "She shouldn't be."

Duane forged towards Donald, his hand sweeping across Donald's face in a vicious blow, sending his son back against the wall.

"I did this for you. She belongs to you, not him."

"No, she doesn't. She's his wife, not mine." Donald stared at his father, not understanding what Duane was really saying.

"No, she's yours. She always has been. I brought her here just for that."

Donald stared at his father even harder, horror spending through him, not quite sure what he meant. "Dad, what did you go and do?"

Leah's gaze shifted between the two men and she realized she needed to get away and soon. There was no telling what Duane would do to her and she feared for Josh, not knowing if he was safe. Her fear for Josh intensified as she listened to the ranting and raving of the older man and Donald's horrified responses.

As she listened, her heart broke within her, hearing just what the man had done, and how he had affected her life from such an early age. She finally stood, her eyes searching the room.

Duane spun, storming back at her in a rage, threatening her, telling her to sit back down.

"I need to use the facilities. Please? Let me use them, and I'll come right back." Leah had no intention of doing that, but she needed him to let her go. She had begun to recognize the building, knowing it was one Josh owned and she had been through it with him just recently. She needed to get away and then she could find a place to hide.

Donald finally convinced his father to let her use the facilities, his eyes unreadable as he motioned her to follow him, not realizing she knew the building.

She thanked him as she shut the door and then locked it, finding a chair to jam under the doorknob, and then searching for somewhere to hide. She opened the window, brushing the snow off, to give the illusion she had snuck out that way. It wasn't that far of a drop to the ground, but she wasn't ready to try that, not yet. If she didn't find somewhere soon to hide, she would.

She searched the room, finding nowhere to hide. She shot a look at the door, knowing she needed to made a move soon before the men broke the door down. She clutched each side of the window and prayed for protection of her unborn child. She pulled herself through the window and dropped, sinking to the ground as she felt pain in her leg, her eyes searching around, desperate to find a hiding place. She rose, running as quickly as she could, or hobbling as she thought, for another building, seeking the travelled portion of the street, where her footsteps would be hidden.

She tried a door of an empty building, finding it open. She slipped inside and searched for a hiding place, knowing she would need one and quickly. She hurried for the stairs to the basement and started down, her wet shoes slipping out from under her in her haste. She muffled her scream as she hit the concrete stairs and slid, ending in a crumpled heap at the bottom of the stairs. Pain blinded her and she sank back, her last conscious thought was a prayer for the little one, that the way she had fallen would have protected it.

Hours later she roused as she heard voices talking to her and hands on her. She tried to fight back until she realized it wasn't either Duane or Donald. She relaxed, letting the paramedics assess her and then lift her to a stretcher, wrapping her in blankets to try and warm her. The older one paused as her words, and then nodded.

Leah's mind came back to the present as she heard the door open and Josh and Ed entered her hospital room. She sighed. She just wanted to sleep but it looked as if that would have to wait. They had promised her that she would be taken upstairs to a room shortly. That's all she wanted, to be in a quiet room, with Josh nearby. She had had a rough two days, given what she had learned yesterday and then today. She reached for Josh's hand, but he was not content with just that. He sat on the side of her bed, wrapping her into his arms, his hands finding hers as he studied first her and then Ed.

Chapter 20

ℱd studied the younger couple in front of him. He shook his head as he tried to come up with the words he needed, to find the questions he had to ask. Leah looked exhausted and it was no wonder, given what she had been through in the last couple of days. Simon had shared the news about the DNA results and that the detective on the other coast had talked to her biological parents, who wanted to fly out that night. Simon had in turn spoken with them and had convinced them to wait for a couple of days and then to come.

"Ed?" Leah's quiet voice broke into his thoughts.

"Leah, how are you feeling?"

"Sore. Exhausted. I just want this all over with, Ed. Can you do that?"

"I will do my best. I just need you to tell me what happened today." He watched as her eyes slid closed and her hands gripped

236

Josh's tighter. "If it's okay with you, I'd like to tape it. Then I'll have your statement transcribed, bring it to you and have you go over it and sign it."

"I can, but it's difficult. It affects someone who lived and worked in this town, and I'm still not sure how far he is involved in this." She looked up at Josh, at a loss for words for a moment. She prayed hard, knowing it would be God's strength that got her through what she had to say. She didn't know how either man would take what she had to say.

She sighed, knowing she had to start way back, when she was small and give Ed the information Simon had given her.

"Did Simon talk to you, Ed?" When he nodded, she sighed. "Thank God for that. I don't want to go back to that, but I have to. That's where it all starts." She blinked back tears as Josh's arms tightened around her, not sure where she was going with her words.

"Duane Alberts is the one who abducted me today. He worked at my last workplace. He's the one I was running from. I didn't know why at the time or what he had really done.   Donald is his son. Donald has his mother's name, his parents not being married."   She looked up, gathering strength to continue.

"Duane apparently abducted me years ago, when I was three, and brought me to this side of the country. He arranged for the sitter that my parents hired, all with this devious plot in mind. He knew who my father's ancestors were. He decided that I would grow up, marry Donald, and Duane would live off the inheritance he knew my father had coming to him."

"Wait!   You said Duane Alberts? Donald's his son?" Ed looked up from his notes. "Duane's been on our radar for years. We just haven't been able to prove anything against him. Now, thanks to you, we can." He looked down at his notes. "What else, Leah?"

Leah continued to talk, her voice low at times.   Ed finally tucked his notebook away as well as the dictator, knowing his night was not yet over. "Have you any idea where they might be now?"

She shook her head.   "I asked the officer who found me but he didn't see them.   He said he hadn't planned on searching that building but something made him."   She leaned back against Josh, suddenly exhausted beyond what she had ever been. Her eyes closed and she slept.

Ed looked up to ask a question, his words dying on his lips as he watched Josh cradling his wife, his eyes on her face. Ed walked quietly from the room, meeting a nurse heading that say.

"She's sleeping, Nance."

"I thought she would be.   We're moving her upstairs. I don't suppose Josh will be heading home any time soon."

Ed started to laugh. "I highly doubt you'll get him to let her out of his sight. At least not for tonight."

Josh stood, watching as the nurses settled Leah into her new room, Leah not arousing at all. He walked back towards her, finding a chair to draw close to the bed, his hand reaching for hers. He settled back, not caring how uncomfortable he was, and slept as well, Leah's hand tight in his.

Before he slept he thought through what all Leah had said, the reasoning behind her kidnapping all those years ago, and his heart broke, first for his wife and then for her parents. He thanked God that she had survived today. If she hadn't managed to get away, he doubted that she would have. He was puzzled, though, on how Donald fit into it and if he knew what his father had really been up to.

Lord, You know. You know the outcome of this and the reasoning why. I hurt for Leah and her parents, for her foster parents and their daughter. But I am thankful she came here, that she's mine. My life would be empty without her. Please, dear Lord, we need Your strength to get through the next few days. Help the authorities to find Duane and Donald quickly before any more harm is done.

His head rested back on the pillow tucked behind his head and he slept, Leah's hand tucked tightly in his. He didn't hear the door swish open and a man enter. Old Jack stood at the foot of the bed for a moment, his eyes assessing his young friends, before he nodded and walked away. He knew where Donald was hiding. He was headed there to find him and convince him to turn himself in.

Chapter 21

Leah laughed at the antics of Heidi as she crawled up to cuddle beside her on her hospital bed. Joy had brought Heidi in to see her Aunt Leah at the little girl's insistence. Heidi plopped down tight to Leah, with Leah's arm around her as she placed her picture book on her bent knees and began to tell her aunt a story.

Somewhere in the midst of the story, Heidi's words shocked her mother and made Leah laugh.

"You need to have a baby, Aunt Leah."

Leah's caught back the giggles that wanted to burst from her, sharing an amused glance with Joy. They hadn't told anyone yet, waiting until the timing was right.

"And why should I?"

Heidi shrugged. "Just because. You and Uncle Josh need a baby. Then I'd have someone else to play with at your place."

Joy struggled to hold back her own giggles. "Heidi, I think we need to go. Say goodbye to Aunt Leah. Uncle Josh said he'd stop by later if he could. Remember, you have something to finish for him."

"Oh I do. I do." Heidi scrambled from the bed, her book flying through the air, forgotten, as she headed for her jacket. "Bye, Aunt Leah. I'll be back."

Joy shook her head. "And Aunt Leah is saying that's what she's afraid of. Sorry, Leah. I have no idea where she came up with that."

"It's okay, Joy. It's understandable. Aren't married couples supposed to have families?" Leah laughed at the look on Joy's face. "Go. Josh says he'll stop in before the girls go to bed. Thanks for coming."

Leah laid back on her pillows, her thoughts on the little girl and her questions before she reached for her Bible. She was behind on her readings and missed the strength she drew from each's day Scripture.

She looked up later as the door opened and a head peeked around it. Simon stood there, hesitating before he entered.

"Simon. Hi. You can come in, you know." Laughter filled Leah's words.

"Leah. How are you today?"

She shrugged, her eyes on his face. "I'm fine. Going home tomorrow, thank goodness. But you didn't come here to discuss my health, now did you?"

He grinned at her. "You found me out. Not that I wasn't interested in how you were feeling." He drew up a chair, after handing her a thick envelope. "Here. Your biological parents asked that I give you this. They are in town, but won't come near you until you have read this and have talked to Josh. They are eager to see you, but will understand if you would rather not see them."

Leah's hand rubbed against the envelope. "Thank you, Simon, for what you have done. This will help. I gather it's letters, photos, whatever I need to try and bridge a years-long gap in our history. I do want to see them, but not here. Somewhere neutral and safe."

"That's what I thought you'd say. Jeremiah has suggested that you use a room at the church. The board is in agreement on that."

"Bless him. He's always thinking one step ahead of everyone, isn't he?" She looked up, tears sparkling in her eyes for a moment. "I could be very angry and at times I have had to damp that down. If I had not been kidnapped, I would not have met Josh or any of his friends. My life would be empty without all of you in it. Thank you, Simon, for caring so much, even when you knows it will hurt."

Simon just nodded, fighting back his own emotions. They talked for a while longer before he hugged her and walked away, stopping in the hallway outside her door to lean against the wall, his eyes closing as he prayed for a lady of his own. He saw the happiness his three friends had now and desired that for himself. Help me to be content, Lord, in whatever place You put me.

Josh walked in on Leah an hour later, finding her still sitting with her hands on the envelope, having made no move to open it. She had spent the time in prayer, seeking wisdom and understanding. He kissed her, then looked down at the envelope.

"What's this, sweetheart?"

"Simon was by. This is from my biological parents. They wanted me to have this and look it over before we meet. Jeremiah has offered a room at the church for that."

"That would be good. The prayer room, I think, would be the best one."

She nodded, her face pensive. "Do I really want to do this, Josh? Meet them? I know it wasn't their fault, but it all is so horrible for us. Will wounds be opened up that shouldn't be? It all ties back to Mistletoe and that town charter."

Josh perched himself beside her and wrapped an arm around her, pulling her to him. "It does. But it also goes to Duane's greed. He wanted something that wasn't his to have and he used you to try and get it. He also used Donald."

"Ed was by earlier. Did he talk to you?" Leah tilted her head back to look up at Josh.

"He stopped by but I was too busy to talk. What did he have to say?"

"Apparently, Old Jack found Donald and convinced him to turn himself in. What a mess that is! He wasn't the one who sent Julia and Blackie out that day. He wasn't in town, moving away because of his father. Duane hired a lookalike, figuring in the heat of the moment, no one would notice the slight differences."

"Julia mentioned later that something seemed off about him. Now we know why."

She nodded. "Donald wasn't sure why, but he thinks his father tried to get Julia to marry Donald and she refused."

"That makes sense, in a weird way, I think." Josh looked down at the envelope. "So, do we open this or not?"

"I want to wait until I'm home. There are too many interruptions here. Doc says I'm being released tomorrow."

"I'm glad. The house has been empty without you."

They talked for a while longer before Josh finally stood, his back to the door. "I need to run for a while. I promised Joy's girls I wold stop by. I'll be back." He stared at Leah as she started to giggle. "What did I say that was so funny?"

"Not you. Heidi. Joy and Heidi were here earlier. Heidi has decided we need to have a baby because then she'd have someone besides Holly to play with."

Josh broke out into laughter. "Our little logician. What next?"

Leah shrugged. "Who knows? I'm just glad it's almost over, Josh. I'm ready to move on, to meet my parents and get to know them, and to reunite with Mom and Dad Whitley."

Engrossed in their talk, neither heard the door swish quietly open or see the man who entered. A movement had Leah looking up, then screaming at Josh to duck.

Josh partly turned, but not enough to avoid the vicious blow that slammed into his head and shoulders, sending him first into Leah's bed and then to the floor, where he laid in a scrawled heap.

Leah's horrified eyes stared at Duane as he stood, club in hand, watching to ensure that Josh didn't move, before he looked at her, an evil grin on his face.

"Now, my girl, it's time to deal with you. You're coming with me. We'll end this now."

Leah scrambled off the other side of the bed, inching away from Duane, her eyes on him, terror rushing through her. She knew what he was hinting at. She wouldn't survive this time. He meant to kill her. And that she would not allow to happen.

She inched along the wall, seeing a slight movement from Josh that drew Duane's attention. She flew for the door, yanking it open and flying down the hall, seeing hospital security running her way. Her scream when Josh had been hit had alerted them that something was desperately wrong.

One of them caught her into his arms and turned, running with her towards an empty room, where he deposited her on the bed, Doc and a nurse behind him.

Sobs rent through the air as her words tumbled over each other, letting them know that Josh was hurt and that Duane was in there with him, that he wanted to kill her.

Doc tried to reassure her that the police were on their way, that Josh would be okay. She just kept shaking her head, sobs increasing with each breath. Doc turned as Abby Waters, the obstetrician, entered the room, fetal monitor in tow.

"We need to calm her down, Abby. She's refusing any medications, but we need to give her something."

"A mild sedative will be fine, I think. Can we get her laying back, do you think?"

Doc shook his head. "She's absolutely refusing to do just that. She's fighting us." He turned to the nurse, giving an order for a mild sedative. "We need that stat, nurse."

She nodded, running for the door and then the head nurse, who was already on her way to the medication cabinet. The nurse returned, handing the syringe to Doc, who quickly administered it, Leah not even aware of what he had done. Leah finally calmed as the sedative took affect, laying back and closing her eyes. Abby watched her, then moved for the monitor, turning as she heard a commotion in the hallway.

Doc nodded at her and then headed for the door, asking the nurse to stay where she was.

Duane had turned as he heard the door shut, seeing for the first time that Leah had escaped him once again. Rage engulfed him as he stumbled around the room, foam flying from his mouth as he sputtered profanity, before he stood over Josh, seeing that he wasn't moving.

He raged around the room, his words becoming more incoherent the longer he talked, his feet stumbling over one another. Josh watched quietly from where he lay, gathering strength to move. His head and shoulder pounded with pain and he wasn't sure he would be able to even get up.

He watched as Duane finally stood at the window, hands braced on the glass, the club he had been holding dropped on the floor near Josh. Josh reached carefully for it, knowing he would need to defend himself in some way against Duane. He rose as silently as he could and backed towards the door, not realizing that Duane would see him in the glass.

Duane spun and charged for him, anger spewing from him. Josh swung the club, catching Duane on a knee and sending him crashing to the floor, his head thudding in a hollow sound. Josh stood for a few seconds, then ran for the door, pulling it open and running through, right into the arms of the Emergency Task Force officers gathered outside the room. He was quickly moved from the area, towards the room where Leah lay.

Doc looked at him and pointed to a chair.

"Sit, Josh. Let's see how much damage that thick head of yours took." Doc grinned at the look Josh shot him.

"It hurts, Doc, but I've had worse." He tried to peek around the physician, searching for Leah. "Leah?"

"She's sleeping, Josh. We had to give her something to calm her down. She just wouldn't stop. And yes, Abby Waters has been in. The baby's fine." He felt Josh's head and then shoulder. "Nothing broken, but it'll bruise. We'll ice it now and I suggest you ice it every three to four hours as best you can. You won't be using that arm much for a few days." He nodded towards a room door. "Now, go. Find your wife. Given what's happened, I think we'll let her go home today." He turned as an officer approached, a large envelope in hand. "This is addressed to Leah."

Josh reached for it. "It's hers. Simon dropped it off earlier." Josh kept his eyes on it for a moment before he raised them to Doc. "Pray for her, Doc. This is from her biological parents. They want to meet with her."

"I have been, Josh." He patted the younger man on his shoulder. "Now, go find your wife. It will all work out. Trust me. God is in control, even when it looks as if evil will win."

He turned and walked away, knowing he was needed to look at Duane. He stopped as Ed approached him, an unreadable look on his face. A few words and Doc nodded, before continuing on his way towards the room.

Chapter 22

*S*unday found Josh and Leah curled up on the couch, the envelope in her hands, his arm around her. Knowing how hard this was for her, Josh prayed for them, waiting as she fingered the flap before opening it and pulling out the sheaf of papers.

"This is hard, Josh. How hard has it been for them all these years, not knowing? I don't even know if they are believers, having God's comfort through all this."

He nodded at the paperwork. "I think that will tell you. Do you want me to start?"

She shook her head. "No, thank you. I have to. I'm just glad you're here, that I have someone with me."

She picked up an envelope, the one on top, and opened it, seeing a birthday card for a four-year-old. Birthday cards, Christmas cards, just-because cards, were next. She read them, then Josh took them from her, watching as she had to pause every once in a while to wipe away the tears.

She fingered through the photos, seeing her early childhood, then photos of her parents through the years. It saddened her that knowing and loving them had been taken from her.

She finally came to a long envelope and hesitated, her hand tracing the name on it. "Leah Rebekah. At least my name is the same. They didn't change that." She looked up, her gaze going towards the front window, seeing the early signs of spring in the buds on the trees. "Josh. I'm afraid. I don't know why."

Josh's lips thinned for a moment as he thought about what Leah had been through for most of her life. "It's understandable, Leah. This is an unknown for you. You've wanted to meet your parents but had no idea who they are or if they even wanted you. That you were stolen never likely crossed your mind." He hugged her tighter, her hands coming up to clasp his arms. "Do you want me to read it for you?"

Tears blocked her vision as she nodded. "Please." Her voice was barely audible.

Josh took another moment to pray aloud for them before he reached for the envelope, setting it aside as he drew a blanket up and over Leah, seeking to bring her warmth and comfort.

He still hesitated as he looked at the envelope before he opened it and unfolded the pages within it, knowing that once it was read, it would change their lives. He prayed they would be ready for that.

"Dearest Leah, our beloved daughter

"It was with fearful hearts we took that call all those months ago that someone fitting your description had been found, on the other side of the country at that. Our hearts raised with hope as we heard that DNA needed to be tested in order to prove that our hopes were real and that you had finally been found.

"You will never know the anguish and pain we felt when we were told you had drowned. That we never ever believed. Our prayer has been that you were alive and well taken care of.

"When we got a call from a detective named Simon, who said he was a friend of yours, and confirmed what detective here had told us, that you were our daughter and that you were alive and well and happily married, our hearts almost burst with happiness and joy. We wanted to come that night but your friend asked that we wait for a couple of days. That allowed us time to prepare what was in this envelope for you, to help you to see and understand us better. It didn't help prepare us to meet you. That can't be done. Not after all these years. The only thing that can prepare us is to actually see you.

"Your friend said you were raised in a loving home with foster parents who so wanted to adopt you but were refused at every turn. You will never know our sorrow at knowing it was because of an inheritance your father never knew about. He lost his father at an early age and never knew his roots, not until now.

"We are in town, and would dearly love to meet you and your husband, Josh I think Simon said his name was. Whenever it feels right for you, let Simon know. He will arrange for us to meet.

"Just know that we have loved you so much all these years and have grieved the loss of the bright and loving daughter you were even at a young age. We have prayed daily for you as has our church family over the years. They were so overjoyed to hear that you are alive and well and happy.

"Love your mother and father."

Leah buried her head against Josh as he finished. "This is just too cruel, for Duane to have done this to them. How could he?"

"Greed, sweetheart. It all comes down to greed. And now he has to answer, not to earthly authorities but to God." Josh had received word that Duane had died the previous night, an undiagnosed brain tumour taking his life. "He wouldn't have lived to stand trial anyway."

"I know, but there are still so many unanswered questions."

"Not really. Ed talked to me at church this morning, just long enough to say that Duane had kept journals over the years, and that what he said about kidnapping you to have you marry Donald was true. He had a sick and twisted mind. He had even decided that if Donald wouldn't marry you, he'd force you to marry himself."

Leah stared at Josh in horror. "That is just so sick. How cruel and how evil!"

Josh nodded. "We'll never know exactly what he was thinking in those last few days. But his journals indicate that he got rid of the woman who helped him. He gave a location and the authorities are searching that area now, likely to find her remains where he said."

Leah shuddered, her head back on Josh's shoulder. "There is just so much evil in the world, Josh. This town has so much hope and good in it. The town founders looked after it all in such a legal manner but there are still those who want it all, to whom it doesn't belong."

"There will always be people like that." Josh hesitated, before he continued. "Do you want to meet with your parents?"

She nodded. "Jeremiah suggested Wednesday afternoon. They have agreed to that, if we agree. I said we'd let him know after we talked."

"We'll plan on that. Now, let's pray, Leah. We'll need God's strength to get us through the next few days." He paused. "What about your foster parents?"

"They're on board. I talked to them earlier today. They want to meet my parents as well, but that will be on another day."

Wednesday found Leah pacing the prayer room at the church, uncertainty in her very movements. Josh leaned against a wall, his eyes on his wife, not knowing how to comfort her in this situation, but knowing she was hurting in more ways than one.

Leah looked up to find Josh watching her and moved quickly to him, welcoming his hug as he wrapped her tight into his arms, his head on hers, a prayer rising between them. Josh looked up as the door opened and Jeremiah entered.

"They're here?" Josh's quiet words had Leah turning in his arms to study him. "What's wrong, Jeremiah?"

Jeremiah just shook his head. "Leah looks so much like her, it's spooky." He paused, at a loss for words. "Are you ready?"

"No. I'm not, but we need to do this." Leah's voice was quite but filled with fear.

Jeremiah nodded as he approached. "Then, as your pastor and also as your family, let me pray with you and for you and for them."

Leah watched as the door opened and a couple entered, her breath coming in a quick gasp as she saw what Jeremiah meant. She really did look like the woman.

Awkwardness was the order of the moment, until Josh stepped in, a hand going out to greet the couple. The woman finally stood, hands on her face as tears flowed.

"Leah!   Oh my!   How God has protected you all these years!   You are so beautiful!"

That broke the silence and they finally sat on the couches in the corner. Jeremiah had made sure to have refreshments available if they needed them.

Silence reigned for a few minutes, until Josh began to ask the questions Leah and he had talked about.

Two hours later, Leah sat between her parents, gripping their hands, tears on their faces, and laughter sounding through the room. Josh sat back, satisfied that Leah was loved by this couple who had missed out on so much with her.

Jeremiah peeked in and then entered, coming to sit near them, not saying anything, but happiness on his face.

"Everything's okay, Jeremiah. Thank you." Leah shared a look with Josh. "We still have a lot of work to do, but Mom and Dad have said they are willing to move here. They're both retired and have nothing to hold them on the other coast now."

"That's correct, Pastor Jeremiah. We have already sold our house, having planned to move somewhere else anyway. Now that Leah is settled here, and I understand I have an inheritance in this town I didn't know about, we're happy to move here." Joseph Bronagh shared a look with his wife. "We both want this, but the final decision rests with Leah."

"I want you here. The Whitleys live about two hours from here, so we can keep in contact. I want you to meet them." She suddenly yawned, exhaustion in her very voice and movements.

Josh stood, reaching to gather her close. "I think I need to take her home. She's had a rough few days. Thank you, Joseph. Anna. I'll call you later today."

They watched as Josh walked away, Leah almost asleep in his arms, knowing she was treasured and loved by so many.

$Epilogue$

Eight months later, Simon smiled as he watched Josh and Leah move among their family and friends. God has blessed them, he thought, before moving forward to shake Josh's hand and drop a kiss on Leah's cheek, before looking down at the bundle Josh cradled so carefully and close to his heart.

Josh's eyes followed Simon's, to study his sleeping daughter. Rebecca was the image of her mother, to his delight. His finger reached to touch the dark red hair and then his hand reached for Leah's. He was blessed, he thought, thinking of the treasures God had provided for him, Leah and now Rebecca.

They had gone through a lot, Leah thought, watching Josh and their daughter, knowing how much she was loved and just how much he loved their little one. She had had a difficult life, that was a given, but God had blessed her as well. First with a foster family that loved her deeply and had raised her in the Christian faith. Then with Josh, a Godly man who loved her more than she ever dreamed of being loved. And now with their daughter. And being reunited with her parents. Her heart seemed fuller as she felt an arm around her shoulders and her father stood there, her mother beside Josh. She heard a camera click somewhere and smiled. Yes, God had been good to them.

Ed had talked to them earlier that day. It had taken months to finally unravel the web Duane had constructed, but what he had told them was that Duane had been determined to become one of the members of the founding families of Mistletoe, that he decided he needed the money and buildings that came to the heirs.

Donald had helped to unravel that web, but even he had not known the extent of his father's deceit or that he had had a woman murdered. He had cooperated with the authorities and then walked away from Mistletoe, knowing he was not welcome there anymore. He had spoke with Blackie and Julia and then Josh and Leah, apologizing for his father and trying to make amends. The two couples had taken his apologies and then suggested he find God, that that would be the only way he would ever have peace. He had listened to them, talked with Jeremiah, and then walked away.

Leah turned as Heidi and Holly ran towards them, the little girls delighted that Josh and Leah had a baby girl. Though a boy would have been welcome, Heidi acknowledged, not understanding the laughter of the adults as she said that.

Leah's eyes lifted to where her foster parents and foster sister were talking with Josh's parents. She looked up as Josh's arm cradled her close to him, his eyes on her before he kissed her, his other arm still cradling his daughter.

"God has blessed us, sweetheart. He protected us and brought people back into your life that you had lost." He smiled as she blinked back tears.

"He has at that, love. Perhaps now we can have a quieter life. God has provided for us and our families." She rested her head on his shoulder, her eyes on Rebecca, not seeing the photographer hired by her parents to take photos of the baby dedication

set up and take the perfect family shot for
them.

Dear Readers:

Thank you for picking up the story of Josh and Leah, the third in the Mistletoe series. Josh was very determined from the outset on how he was to meet Leah and what would happen to them. Leah was just as determined that Josh needed that little kitten. While working on this story, it has come close to Christmas and a time of year that brings to mind God's gift to us.

Greed plays a huge role in our world today. People are not satisfied with what they have, wanting more and more, not realizing that the best thing in life is God's love and His provision for us, that we can live with Him forever.

Josh's favourite verse is also one of mine - to be strong and of good courage. It is not a coincident that his verse comes from a book that shares his name, the book of Joshua.

As you travel through life, cherish those treasures God has given you: your

family, friends, other loved ones. They are
never with us long enough.

God bless.

Ronna

www.ingramcontent.com/pod-product-compliance
Lightning Source LLC
Chambersburg PA
CBHW070441200726
48293CB00007B/2104